# Darrow's Badge

Sapphires, rubies, pearls and diamonds: to Sir Hugh Keating, English aristocrat and Govan town deputy, the jewellery is the dowry for his future wife. To Black Elliot and his gang, however, the jewellery means money and prestige. So, when the gems are stolen, it means a lot of trouble for Sheriff Darrow.

Somehow he must prevent the jewellery from being smuggled out of Govan and he and his men are stretched to their limits as they guard the trails and search the town. Meanwhile, Black Elliot must stay one jump ahead of the law as he fights to keep his men under control.

Darrow's right to wear his badge is under threat and as time runs out for both men, the battle of wits will finish in a cloud of gunsmoke.

# Darrow's Badge

GILLIAN F. TAYLOR

A Black Horse Western

ROBERT HALE · LONDON

© Gillian F. Taylor 2005
First published in Great Britain 2005

ISBN 0 7090 7745 9

Robert Hale Limited
Clerkenwell House
Clerkenwell Green
London EC1R 0HT .

Typeset by
Derek Doyle & Associates, Shaw Heath.
Printed and bound in Great Britain by
Antony Rowe Limited, Wiltshire

# CHAPTER ONE

The striped canvas awning out front of V. Crane's Drug Store made the sidewalk a shady place to sit on a hot June morning. Black Elliot had taken one of the plain wooden seats there and was sipping on a root beer as he watched the bustle on Main Street, Govan, Wyoming. Less obviously he was also watching the front of the sheriff's office, on the opposite side of the dusty street. The railroad town had boomed dramatically in the last year, and there had been plenty of money invested. Black Elliot fancied having some of that money, so he'd come to Govan with three accomplices, to see how best to get it. To Elliot's mind, success lay in making plans and sticking by them, not going off on some half-baked idea. He liked to survey a town he planned to rob, and take a look at the local law.

The screen door of the sheriff's office opened at last. Elliot had strolled past earlier, and noted that the sheriff's name was B. Darrow. The man coming out now had to be him; his air of authority told as much as the shield-and-crescent badge on the lapel of his smart, black jacket. Black Elliot guessed that

Sheriff Darrow was in his late thirties, a dark-eyed, handsome man and difficult to read. Darrow answered a greeting from a man passing on the sidewalk, as he closed the screen door. Elliot noticed that he didn't smile. He also noticed that the sheriff wore a long-barrelled Army Colt holstered at his side. A lumber wagon blocked Elliot's view across the street briefly as it went by. When the road was clear again, the sheriff was walking briskly towards the crossroads. Other townsfolk nodded and spoke respectfully to him, though none seemed downright friendly. Black Elliot watched the sheriff round the corner into Cross Street, and pass from his view.

He finished his root beer and felt in his pocket for the harmonica he always carried with him. It was a habit to play the harmonica softly while he thought. The sheriff looked smart, and competent enough, but Black Elliot was sure he was smarter. Something else encouraged him to pit himself against the sheriff. He hadn't been able to make out exactly what Darrow had said, but Elliot had recognized his accent. It went with the self-confidence and touch of arrogance that Elliot had seen years before in men like Darrow. The sheriff was a Southern aristocrat; a man born to own land and slaves, and still aware of that, no matter what had happened to him since the War Between the States. Black Elliot was a half-caste, and had suffered for it in past years. He bitterly resented the difference between what life had offered to Darrow, and his own, harder lot. Elliot came to a decision: he would take on Sheriff Darrow, and make the man regret ever pinning on a law badge.

\*

Someone else had also been waiting for Sheriff Darrow. His deputy was waiting for him at the far side of the new footbridge that crossed the river circling to the west of town. Hugh Talbot Keating, old boy of Harrow, graduate of Cambridge University, second son of Sir Waldon John Keating, Bart., was slouching against a tree, with his hands in his trouser pockets. A wide-brimmed hat hid the fact that his golden-brown hair was rather thin at the front. His dark eyes were softer than Darrow's, and he had an air of harmlessness that seemed at odds with the heavy Webley revolver holstered at his waist. Hugh didn't like the gun, but in a crisis he was an excellent shot.

As Darrow approached, Hugh Keating straightened himself.

'It's nothing like a travelling fair at home,' he complained, in his upper-class English accent. 'Our stalls are beautiful: wooden ones, all carved and painted. Red and gold, lots of gold. And mirrors.' Darrow didn't bother stopping as Hugh spoke, forcing his deputy to hurry to catch up. 'These booths are nothing but wood frames and painted canvas. And you do have peculiar names for your stalls.'

'Such as?' Darrow answered, his nose wrinkling in distaste at the smell from the roasted-sausage stall which was the nearest to them as they approached the carnival.

'Ring-Toss,' Hugh promptly replied. 'That's a Hoop-La. And you call a Test-Your-Strength-Machine, a Hi-Striker!'

'No matter what they are called, the question is, how many of them will be illegally rigged?' Darrow knew nothing about how such games worked, legally or otherwise. He had only been mildly surprised when Hugh had claimed to know what to look for. His deputy had already proved his skill at juggling, magic tricks, card-handling and even lock-picking in the past.

The main street of the carnival had roughly half a dozen stalls and tents on either side, offering a variety of excitements and games. At the far end was the Tent of Wonders, the tent itself hidden behind gaudy painted canvas screens showing dramatic representations of the world-beating attractions within. To the right of the main street was a second street of booths, running parallel with the main one but with only four stalls on each side. The Hall of Mirrors stood at the top of this street, separated from the Tent of Wonders by a small booth selling cold drinks.

As it was only late morning, finishing touches were still being put on the stalls. The prizes were being arranged on the shelves as Darrow and Hugh arrived at the Over-Under stall. For this game, the player could roll six balls down the board to finish in slots with values from one to six. Totals of under eleven or over thirty won a prize. Hugh picked up one of the balls and rolled it towards the six slot, which was third from right. It hit the edge of the slot and bounced left into the number one slot. The stall's operator turned round from tightening one of the stall's guy ropes.

'What in hell are you doin'?' he exclaimed. 'You

gotta pay afore ye play.'

Darrow stared at the stall owner and indicated the crescent-and-shield badge of office pinned to his jacket.

'We're here to see that the good people of this town only play against the regular odds.'

Hugh picked up another ball and tried again; this one went neatly into the slot.

'I think it's all right.'

'Damn sure it is, buster.' The man's sun-reddened face was drawn into a tight scowl.

'In that case, you got no reason to get sore about us checking it,' Darrow pointed out.

The next stall was a cane rack game. Canes of all varieties were stuck through a canvas stretched over a frame. *The cane you ring is the cane you win*, explained the flowery boards either side. Hugh picked up a wooden hoop and lobbed it at a cane with a large curved handle. He would have ringed it but the ring wasn't quite large enough to pass over the handle; it tilted to one side and slipped off. Darrow had already seen the small notice at the back of the booth that explained that rings had to pass over the cane and land on the canvas in order to win.

'I'd sure admire to test this, iffen you don't mind,' he said to the stall owner. His eyes suggested that the owner's opinion didn't matter much anyway. Darrow pulled the cane from the canvas and tried another ring: it would not fit over the curved handle. Darrow threw the cane back at the stall owner. 'I don't want to see any of these out on the stall while you're in my town. Is that clear?'

'Aw, easy now, Sheriff,' the owner said placatingly. He rubbed the back of his knuckle against his stubbly cheek. 'I gotta make a living, and if folks are dumb enough to try throwing a small ring over a large cane, that's only five cents they've wasted.' He stood alongside the sheriff. 'I can't make them read that sign now, can't I? Them canes bring me an extra . . . ten dollars a week?'

'That sounds like bribery,' Darrow drawled. 'For attempting to rig a stall, and bribe an elected officer of the law, I reckon a fine of twenty dollars should cover things.' He held out his hand. Neither Darrow nor Hugh missed the brief look of pain in the stall operator's eyes, but the man got out his wallet and handed over the notes. Darrow put the money away in his own wallet and eyed the cane the stall operator was holding.

'Better put that back, there's some suckers arriving.'

Hugh followed Darrow as they moved to the next attraction. 'What about my share? I'm the one who knows how these things are set up.' His bank balances had taken quite a dent lately, and his conscience had never been too strong with regards to easy money.

'Consider your future wife's reputation,' Darrow answered. 'I'm sure that you would not care for it to be sullied by rumours that her husband has been taking bribes, and from a two-bit showman at that. An officer of the law and prominent citizen of the town should be bribed by somebody with appropriate social status.'

'You mean a lawyer?' Hugh suggested, knowing full well that Darrow had studied law before the Civil War had left his family penniless. The resulting glare had no effect on his glee at getting the best, for once, in their ongoing war of words.

The sheriff chose to rise above the situation by crossing to look at a game on the other side.

'Sure looks like these carnies ain't getting such no easy ride,' Tomcat Billy remarked, the words drawled in a thick Tennessee accent. He'd been taking an early browse around the booths, and had stopped to watch the lawmen.

'For sure an' that English deputy's clever with throwing things,' Irish replied as Hugh deftly snared a couple of the prizes on the ring-toss game, and declared it legitimate.

'If these here booths have got to play honest, no rigging, they ain't goin' to take enough to be worth robbing,' Tomcat said quietly.

Irish shrugged. 'And won't that be depending on what Black Elliot decides?'

Tomcat Billy turned his alert green eyes on the other booths. His nickname was well justified. He walked quietly and gracefully, much like the wild animals of the mountains where he had grown up. He was a little shorter than average, wiry and had close-cropped brown hair that was often slightly ruffled. Apart from his yellow neckerchief, his clothing was all brown, including the belt that held a knife and a short-barrelled Civilian Peacemaker.

His companion, Irish, appeared even larger by

contrast. He was a tall, powerful and fleshy man with pale blue eyes in a mild face that bore a short goatee. His blond hair was long and slightly curly and was normally tied at the back of his neck for convenience. Although he looked like a slow moving ox, he was surprisingly fast in a fight. His long black coat partially concealed the thick leather belt that carried a long, double-edged knife, and his plain Army Colt.

Tomcat pointed to the tent they were passing.

'You could earn some honest bucks in there.'

It was a boxing tent, where members of the public could challenge prize-fighters for cash prizes. Irish grinned. 'I'm after keeping my face the shape it is now.'

Tomcat grinned back. 'C'm on, let's go find the candy-pull stall.'

Darrow and Hugh had reached the Tent of Wonders at the end of the first row. The Bearded Lady was sitting outside in the sunshine, mending a dress. Hugh nodded politely to her and raised his hat. Darrow belatedly remembered to do the same.

'There was a bearded lady with the fair that came to our village every year,' Hugh remembered as they walked on. 'Esmerelda. Nice woman, but got too fond of gin.'

'If that's the kind of company you used to favour, I'm surely not surprised your family packed you off to commit your indiscretions on another continent,' Darrow said. 'Shame it wasn't Australia.'

Hugh ignored him.

He checked the Plinko game, to ensure that the

pins weren't arranged to prevent players from getting the higher scores. The Hi-Striker, Three-In-A-Row and shooting gallery games all passed inspection without trouble. Darrow wondered why his deputy had skipped the Wheel of Fortune, but didn't ask. He followed as Hugh turned back from the shooting gallery at the end of the row, and waited to see what would happen.

'Good morning.' The stall's holder, J. Archer, according to the florid lettering on his signs, welcomed them. Archer was slightly better-dressed than the other carnival folk and had an air of immense self-confidence. 'You'll find nothing wrong with my machine, I promise you that.'

Darrow and Hugh glanced at one another, both noticing the ambiguity of the words.

'Why, let's hope that's for the right reasons,' Darrow drawled.

Archer smiled. 'I wouldn't like to cause trouble to two such well-respected officers of the law.'

Hugh swelled at the praise, smiling happily.

'And we're here to do a job,' Darrow reminded them. He nudged his deputy. 'So get on with it.'

Hugh glared at him, then moved to examine the back of the Wheel of Fortune machine. He looked carefully at the axle of the wheel. Rigged wheels had a friction brake on the axle, that could be controlled by a pedal or handle. A well-designed machine could be converted from rigged to legal in a matter of seconds, and Archer had had over half an hour's notice of the lawmen's search. There was nothing wrong with Archer's machine, but he lost his air of satisfaction when the deputy produced a magnifying glass and used it to examine the axle and surrounding woodwork in more detail.

'It's worn in all the right places,' Hugh announced, straightening up. 'It's been rigged regularly, and recently.'

Archer was taken completely by surprise. He hadn't considered the wear marks that the brake would leave on the equipment.

'I'm arresting you for possession of illegal property,' Darrow told the showman.

'You haven't any proof,' Archer said defiantly. He smiled again, but the warmth wasn't in his eyes as before. 'But I'm sure you don't want to cause a fuss. Perhaps we can come to some arrangement?'

'I doubt it,' Darrow answered. 'That's a handmade suit you're wearing, and a for-real gold watch—chain across your belly. House odds weren't good enough for you; you've been cheating folk for years.'

All of Archer's charm vanished suddenly.

'I'll sue you for wrongful arrest. I've got friends in government; you'll lose your badge.'

'I've been told that afore now,' Darrow drawled, unimpressed. 'Cuff him,' he told Hugh.

Hugh stepped towards Archer as he reached for the handcuffs in his jacket pocket. He saw the punch thrown at him with just enough time so it struck his cheek, rather than his nose.

'Ow!' Hugh stumbled backwards, dropping the handcuffs.

Darrow managed to dodge him and sprinted towards Archer as he turned to run.

'Stop!' Darrow yelled.

Archer stopped dead as the sheriff was right behind him, and rammed his elbow backwards into Darrow's stomach. As the sheriff gasped, Archer turned and aimed a punch at his face. Darrow ducked and twisted, taking the blow on his shoulder.

'Hold it!' The shout was accompanied by the unmistakable sound of a revolver's hammer being drawn back. Hugh had his Webley pointed directly at Archer's chest and looked angry enough to use it.

'Goddam limey lord!' Archer yelled, his fists still bunched. His face was flushed red. 'What business have you got taking up an American's job?'

'At least I'm doing some good, and not cheating my own people,' Hugh snapped back. 'And I am *not* a lord!'

This last provoked laughter from the few towns-folk within earshot; Hugh's touchiness on the subject was well known.

Archer thought that he was the one being laughed at.

'I'll make you pay for this, you aristocratic son-of-a bitch. This country doesn't belong to you and your sort any more.' His face was twisted with spite.

'That's enough.' Darrow had picked up the dropped handcuffs. Careful not to get between Hugh and Archer, he approached the angry man. Seeing no alternative, Archer allowed himself to be cuffed.

'Justice Robinson doesn't like cheats and scoundrels,'

Hugh told Archer smugly.

Archer took a step towards him, his blue eyes gleaming with hate. Darrow was holding on to the cuffs and brought him up sharply as Hugh took a step backwards and reached for the gun he had holstered.

'I'll get even,' Archer hissed.

Hugh's eyes were round with fear. 'You can't!' he blustered. 'I'm an officer of the law.'

Archer was about to answer when Darrow ordered him to be quiet. The stall-holder kept his mouth shut, but continued to stare at the deputy. Hugh's attention was suddenly diverted by the whistle of the train approaching the station.

'Richard! I'm supposed to meet him!' There was panic in Hugh's voice.

'I can manage,' Darrow said succinctly.

Hugh glanced about, then sprinted towards a man riding a bay horse past the Gypsy Fortune-Teller's booth.

'Stop! Stop!'

The rider reined in his horse and looked around, mildly surprised.

'I need your horse, law business,' Hugh gasped as he ran. He managed to indicate the badge on his jacket.

The rider swung down from the saddle and held out the reins. Hugh grabbed them and vaulted into the saddle, something no one in Govan had ever seen him do before.

'You can pick him up from the railway station,' Hugh yelled to the horse's owner, swinging his borrowed mount around and sending it off at a gallop, almost before he had his feet in the stirrups.

The bay pricked up its ears and galloped on eagerly. Hugh drove it straight for the ford, much to the consternation of a wagon-driver bringing his load in the opposite direction. His horses snorted and half-reared as Hugh galloped past, sending up great splashes of water. Three children playing in the shallow edge of the ford got drenched as the bay bounded past and up on to the bank. Hugh turned right, following the river to the blacksmith's, and turned left into Cross Street. The bay swerved to avoid the laundry's wagon, throwing Hugh forward over its right shoulder. As he struggled to regain his seat, the excited bay charged down the street. Riders hurriedly nudged their mounts aside and a dog that had been scratching itself in the street, leaped up and fled under the sidewalk.

Hugh was in control again as they reached the crossroads. He turned the bay right on to Main Street, the bay adjusting its stride to take the corner. A farmer kicked his solid horse aside as he saw Hugh charging down the street. He yelled a warning which was rapidly heeded. A boy grabbed his younger sister and pulled her on to the sidewalk. Three women who were enjoying a gossip in the middle of the street hitched up their skirts and ran for the sidewalk. Hugh yelled apologies as he passed. A boy of about twelve turned his pony cart too sharply, spilling boxes of tinned goods on to the street. The bay didn't swerve; it hurled itself over the boxes, almost leaving Hugh behind. He caught up the reins as they landed, and sat down in the saddle. Barely in control, he steered around a lumber wagon and galloped on to the railroad depot at the end of the street.

# CHAPTER TWO

Richard Walden Keating, and his wife, Louisa, were standing on the hard-packed, bare soil around the Govan railroad depot. Their trunks, cases, hatboxes and other paraphernalia were being unloaded from the baggage car of the gently steaming train under the supervision of his valet and her maid. Louisa pressed long hat pins deeper into her carefully dressed chestnut hair as the prairie wind tugged at her Parisian hat.

'I told you Hugh would be late, didn't I?' Richard Keating said, glancing about the depot, which consisted of no more than the lumber building that served both as railroad office and the depot manager's-living quarters. There was also a coal shed and a water tower.

'I can't see why Americans won't build platforms at their country stations,' Louisa answered. 'Such a blasted nuisance, having to climb down that little ladder. And in these hoops and skirts,' she added, settling her bustle more comfortably, to the horror of a respectable American matron nearby.

'There seems to be some kind of disturbance up

the street,' Richard observed. 'It must be a cowboy "hurrahing the town".'

'Wherever did you pick up such an expression, Richard?' Louisa shaded her eyes with her gloved hand. 'Actually I think it's Hugh.'

'It couldn't possibly be!' Richard exclaimed as the horse and rider they were watching jumped a pile of boxes.

'No, Richard, I believe I am right,' Louisa said calmly as her brother-in-law raced towards them at a flat-out gallop.

As he got closer, they could see for sure that it was Hugh, who seemed to be having an argument with his horse about stopping. Hugh sat deep in the saddle and gave a sharp tug on the reins. The bay sat on its haunches and slid to a halt three feet in front of Richard and Louisa, who were showered with dust and small stones. Neither of them flinched.

'Sorry,' Hugh gasped. 'Never ridden him before. Not mine.' His hat was gone, his trouser legs were damp from crossing the ford and he was covered in dust. He dismounted and made a futile attempt to brush off some of the dust.

'I'll take him, Hugh,' offered an unkempt and unshaven man who smelt of cheap whiskey.

'Thanks, Pete,' Hugh answered, giving him the horse's reins and a dollar. 'Walk the horse until it's cool, and don't go drinking that until his owner collects him, or I won't send you anything to celebrate my wedding with.'

Richard was about to say something about his brother's acquaintances, but Louisa deflected the inevitable row by getting in first.

'Hugh, dear, didn't you say that your fiancée would be here as well?'

As Hugh looked about, a young woman stepped forward. She had been standing by the depot, but neither Richard nor Louisa had really noticed her. Hugh saw her, smiled, and tried to smooth his wind-blown hair. After apologizing for his late arrival, he introduced her to his family.

'Richard, Louisa, this is my fiancée, Miss Minnie Davis.'

Whatever Richard Keating may have thought of his brother, or his choice of wife, his manners were excellent. He stepped forward and took Minnie's hand.

'I am pleased to meet you,' he said gravely.

'It's very good of you to come all the way out here for our wedding,' Minnie answered modestly. Her delicate green and yellow dress was new and stylish but simpler than Louisa's costly travelling-dress. It suited her, for Minnie was no great beauty, but there was an open freshness in her face that made her more appealing than she realized. Her dusky fair hair was wound into a braided coil on the back of her head and partly hidden under a narrow-brimmed straw hat, trimmed with a green satin ribbon.

'We couldn't miss the opportunity to see the place where Hugh finally intends to settle down and become respectable,' Richard said, grinning at his younger brother.

'That's not what you said at home,' Louisa accused. 'You said it was a good excuse to get in some hunting, and shoot a grizzly, or a buffalo.' She turned to Minnie. 'He just wants to get one up on the others at his club.'

Minnie nodded, and directed a silent appeal for help to Hugh.

Hugh saw her and was about to speak, but got drowned out by the whistle of the train, announcing its imminent departure. Everyone moved a few paces towards the depot building as the engine began to belch out steam and smoke. Richard spoke up while Hugh was still waiting for the noise to die down.

'Is there a wagon or a carriage to take us to the hotel?' he yelled.

Hugh pointed at Pinder's Hotel; it was the nearest building on the other side of Main Street, about thirty feet from the railroad tracks.

'I've booked you rooms there.'

'I could do with stretching my legs a little, after sitting in that train for hours on end,' Louisa said. She led the way across the street, asking Minnie about how long she had lived in Govan and whereabouts her home was. The men followed, Richard taking the chance to annoy Hugh by ruffling his brother's hair. Seen together, their family resemblance was clear, especially in the nose and jawline. However, while Hugh's round, expressive eyes gave him a childlike air, Richard's face was more sharply defined and suggested a greater strength of will.

Minnie and Louisa climbed the steps to the end of the sidewalk outside the hotel. Louisa was asking another question, about why all the buildings were raised above the ground, when she saw that their way was blocked. A heavily built man wearing worn denim trousers and a greying cotton shirt was relaxing in a chair, with his feet propped up on the hitching rail and a bull-whip coiled on his lap. His head was resting against the wall of the hotel and he seemed to be asleep. There was no way to get past him.

Louisa stopped, and coughed loudly. When that failed to get a response, she stepped closer and said, 'Excuse me, may I have room to pass?'

The wagon-driver opened one eye to survey Louisa coolly.

'There's plenty o' room in the street, lady,' he drawled casually.

'I want to get into the hotel, and you are blocking my way,' Louisa retorted icily. 'Kindly move at once.'

'Quit your yapping, an' let a man rest,' the wagon-driver said. 'This damn sidewalk don't belong to you, nohow.'

Louisa let out a loud hiss, rather like an infuriated cat, but before she could do anything, Richard pushed between the two women. In one quick movement, he bent to grab one of the chair's legs, and pulled it out from under the wagon-driver, tumbling him into a heap on the sidewalk.

'You don't speak to my wife like that!' Richard snapped. 'You apologize now.'

But an apology was the last thing on the wagon-driver's mind. He scrambled to his feet, his face flushed a nasty shade of red.

'No damn Limey throws me around!' he yelled. He swung a heavy punch at Richard's face.

The Englishman ducked and threw a sharp jab in return. It connected with the wagoner's nose, causing a roar of fury. He launched a two-fisted attack, which Richard dodged. He was standing lightly, with his hands raised in the style of a trained boxer. As the wagoner recovered his balance, Richard lashed out again with a jab to his opponent's ribs and danced back out of range of a wild swipe.

'He boxed for his college,' Louisa told Minnie proudly, as the women kept out of harm's way at the end of the sidewalk.

'Richard, stop it,' Hugh said loudly.

'I'm going to see that this barbarian gets what he deserves,' Richard answered. He took no notice of the crowd that was gathering in the street and on the opposite sidewalk. He landed another couple of quick blows, to whoops of appreciation from some boys sitting further along on the hitching rail.

The wagon-driver cursed loudly, feinted with his right hand, and caught Richard a heavy blow on the ribs with his left. As Richard gasped, Hugh stepped forward.

'Stop it,' he said again. 'I'm an officer of the law.'

The wagoner replied by aiming a punch that caught Hugh on the side of the jaw; a spot that was already sore from his altercation with the carnival stall-holder. Hugh gave a yell of pain and stumbled against the hitching rail.

'I'm going for help,' Minnie told Louisa. She hitched up her skirts, jumped down from the sidewalk and hurried away along the street.

Louisa did her part by grabbing Hugh's collar and

pulling him away from the fight. Richard and the driver were piling into one another with grim determination. Richard's fine shirt had come untucked and was splattered with blood from his opponent's nose. His hat had fallen off and been trodden on and his hair was falling forward into his eyes. The wagondriver was used to roughhouse brawling, not to facing an opponent who dodged and fought with trained skill. After taking a rapid battery of blows to his ribs, he swore and simply kicked Richard hard on the shin.

Taken by surprise, Richard dropped his defence and took a heavy blow in the stomach. It knocked him backwards into his brother, who had just drawn his gun. Hugh stumbled against the hitching rail and dropped the Webley, which bounced off the edge of the sidewalk into the street below.

'Look what you're doing!' Hugh exclaimed, clinging to the rail as he tried to regain his balance.

'Get out of my way, you fool,' Richard snapped, turning to push his brother away.

Hugh caught his heel and fell backwards, landing heavily on his back. The wagon-driver took the opportunity to punch Richard in the kidneys. Richard gave a yell of pain and tried to turn.

'Fisher! Fisher!' Louisa was calling frantically for her husband's valet, who was supposed to be arranging delivery of the luggage from the station.

As the wagon-driver was bracing himself for another kick, a tall, young man bounded on to the far end of the hotel sidewalk. He seized the driver by his shoulder, and turned him around to deliver a beautiful punch to his jaw. The wagon-driver bounced against the wall of the hotel and collapsed, the fight literally knocked out of him.

'I'm arresting you for assault, and being a public nuisance,' the young man told the dazed driver. He produced a pair of handcuffs and fitted them efficiently

Hugh sat up, complaining to the world in general as he felt his jaw. His brother ignored him, instead giving his attention to the man who had stopped the fight.

'That was an excellent piece of work, officer,' he said. 'I should like to commend you to your superior officer; Sheriff Darrow, I believe?'

'That's right, sir. I'm Deputy Pacey.' The tall young man gave them a warm, bright smile. 'I'm full-time deputy here in Govan now the town's got so large, and Deputy Keating there will only be working part-time after getting married.'

Hugh scrambled to his feet, brushing at his clothes, and glowered at the new deputy. Pacey was ten years younger than himself, over six feet tall, well-built and handsome, with curly brown hair and blue eyes. He had served as a lieutenant in the cavalry, after graduating from a distinguished military college in New England. Finding army life too restrictive, he had decided to try law work. Pacey was a good horseman, a good shot, a good fighter, brave, and popular with women. Hugh had disliked him immediately.

'Take him back to the office and write up the charges in the report book,' Hugh told Pacey, trying to regain some authority.

'Of course.' Deputy Pacey smiled at Richard, then hauled the wagon-driver to his feet and hustled him away along the sidewalk.

'He's just like one of the lawmen in those dime novels that Fisher has been reading since we landed in New York,' Louisa said admiringly.

'He makes an excellent figure of a man,' her husband agreed.

Hugh's opinion that such an excellent figure of a man should be stuffed and used to display clothes, was fortunately silenced by Minnie returning his gun, and asking anxiously how he was. On seeing the bruise forming on his jaw, she insisted on taking him to the sheriff's office, further up the street, to bathe it.

Hugh seized the opportunity to get away from his brother. Taking Minnie's arm, he said goodbye to Richard and Louisa, and left them to check in at the hotel themselves.

'He hasn't been in town five minutes, and he's already managed to make me look useless,' Hugh grumbled. 'Richard always managed to get me into trouble, somehow.'

'Never mind,' Minnie said consolingly. 'We won't be seeing him again until the picnic tomorrow.'

Hugh snorted. 'Life with Richard around is never as simple as a picnic.'

The next morning, Hugh and Minnie met in the entrance of Pinder's Hotel. Minnie was wearing a new royal blue riding habit, and held the folds of the apron awkwardly bunched up.

'Do I look all right?' she asked Hugh.

He looked at his fiancée's anxious face. 'I think this should fasten around here somewhere to form a skirt,' Hugh said, settling the outfit for her. 'You look splendid,' he reassured her. Taking Minnie's arm, he led her upstairs to room 10.

His knock on the door was answered by Fisher, Richard's valet. Pinder's Hotel didn't have a suite as such, but two connecting rooms had been converted for Richard Keating by removing the bedroom furniture from one and substituting drawing-room and parlour furniture rented by special arrangement from the Lotus Furniture Emporium on Judd Street. Inside, they were greeted by Hugh's brother and his wife, and invited to sit down.

'Before we ride, I thought this would be a good opportunity for us to give you your dowry,' Richard explained to Minnie. 'Louisa thought you would want to see it a few days before the wedding, in case you wanted to wear anything, and needed to change your veil, or what-have-you.' He signalled to the maid, who brought forward one of nearly twenty boxes and cases that were piled on a side table. The faded, red leather case held an elaborate pearl necklace, bracelet and earring set.

'These are mine?' Minnie asked, as the case was handed to her. She held it gingerly and stared at the creamy pearls, nestling on red velvet. 'You're giving them to me?'

'They were a wedding present to our grandmother, Georgia-Anne,' Richard told her.

'The one who taught me to play cards,' Hugh added. 'I was very fond of her.'

'And for some reason, she must have been fond of you, because she left most of her jewellery to your future wife,' Richard said. 'At least she had the good sense to say you weren't to be allowed to have it until you got married. You'd have gambled it away in the clubs.'

'I was winning in the clubs,' Hugh protested. 'That's why father asked me to leave. I was doing so well, he thought I must be cheating.'

'Let's see the next piece,' Louisa said firmly. The two men glared at one other and settled down.

The boxes produced a bewildering array of fine jewellery, from earrings to tiaras. Opals, jet, moonstones, garnets, pearls and amethysts all looked rich enough to Minnie as she gingerly handled the beautiful items, but there was more. Gemstones glittered in the sunlight from the windows; the hard brilliance of diamonds and the glow of rubies, emeralds and sapphires. To Minnie, seen all together at once, it looked like pirate's plunder, illustrated in a book.

'Where could I ever wear this?' she asked softly, holding a diamond and ruby necklace.

'The season will have started just before we leave London for Europe,' Hugh told her, referring to their long honeymoon, which was planned to take in France, Switzerland and Italy. 'You'll need things like these for the balls and parties.'

If Hugh's family had feared that Minnie was marrying him for his wealth, her reaction to the richness of the jewellery was enough to reassure them.

'There's also this,' Louisa said, opening another box to show Minnie a simple pearl tiara.

'Oh, that's pretty,' Minnie said, taking it. 'I could wear it for the wedding, although I don't know how to put it with my veil,' she added.

'My maid, Sarah, is very good with hair,' Louisa said. 'I'll send her to your house tomorrow afternoon, so you can try it and see how you want your hair done.'

'But today we're supposed to be going on a picnic,' Richard reminded them. He rose and gave orders for the jewellery to be returned to the hotel safe. 'It's come this far, we don't want to lose it now,' he added.

# CHAPTER THREE

At lunchtime, Irish and Tomcat Billy were in the White Buffalo saloon, with Black Elliot and Curly Joe. Unlike the Main Street saloons, it didn't have a mirror behind the bar; instead it sported a large painting of a naked woman on a *chaise-longue*. The fancy dresses worn by the real women were cut lower in front than elsewhere, with skirts that only reached to the knee. An automatic piano near the stairs rattled out dance tunes and a few men were dancing with saloon girls.

'This is one swell place,' Tomcat remarked. There was a predatory look in his green eyes as he studied the ankles of the nearest hostess.

Black Elliot ignored the comment. 'I think we should forget about the carnival,' he said. He was freshly shaven, well-dressed and smelt faintly of cologne. A gold tooth showed on the few occasions he smiled.

'Less noise and trouble than taking the bank, surely, *amigo*?' Curly Joe asked. He usually went hatless, to show off his black, curly hair. Like Elliot, he too was a dandy, playing up his Mexican heritage with ruffles on his sleeves and a red silk bandanna as a cravat. His neat moustache was carefully trimmed, to add the last touch to his dashing appearance.

'We could only take two or three stalls for sure, even if we split up and acted at the same time,' Elliot said. 'There's no guarantee we'd get the full week's takings.' He took his harmonica from a pocket, and blew a few soft notes. The others waited, knowing that he was planning something. Elliot put the harmonica down and sipped his whiskey.

'Heard any news, aside from the carnival?' he asked.

Curly Joe grinned. 'I heard as some English don had a fight with a man that wouldn't get out of his way. Now me, I'd have put some steel in the bastard.' He replenished his glass from the whiskey bottle they were sharing.

'That Englishman's here because he's brother to the deputy here,' Elliot said. 'That deputy's getting married in a week; it's the talk of the town.'

'Why?' Irish asked. 'What's so special about a deputy getting married now?'

Black Elliot glared at him. 'I don't know and I surely don't care. But I heard tell that half the town's going to be showing off their go-to-meetin' clothes at the church.'

'Which means the town'll be quiet while we do the bank,' Tomcat said softly.

Elliot nodded and picked up his harmonica. 'And iffen we're lucky, then some of those carnival folk will have put their money in the bank.'

Tomcat grinned widely. Elliot played a few more

notes on his harmonica before speaking again.

'Remember to stay out of trouble. Don't do anything to draw attention to you-all. I'll check the place out and fix how we're going to do it.' With that decided, he poured himself a last tot from the whiskey bottle.

A small hand reached over his shoulder and wiped the drip from the neck of the bottle. He turned to see a short, red-haired saloon girl licking the whiskey from her fingers.

'My, a whole tableful of fine gentlemen all to my lonesome self. Do you-all mind if I sit here?' She smiled coyly, making dimples appear in her plump cheeks.

Curly was the quickest to speak. 'Of course you can, Miss . . . ?'

'Amalie.' She bent down to speak her name closer to Curly's ear, affording all the men a clear view of her cleavage. She wore a yellow satin dress, trimmed with black fringes that swung distractingly as she moved. It was cut wide on her shoulders and very low at the front. Her corset pushed her breasts up so they overspilled the edges of the dress. A long gold necklace drew a line across her pale skin from her neck to her breasts.

Curly Joe smiled brilliantly and flicked the fringe hanging from the neck of her dress. Amalie laughed and gave a little shake that sent all the fringes swinging.

'Would you like a drink?' Curly asked, flicking the fringe again.

'Wine, please, *señor*,' she breathed.

Curly stood, bowed to her and went to the bar.

Tomcat Billy jumped to his feet.

'Would you like to dance, Miss Amalie?' he asked, holding out his hand and smiling impishly.

'Why, yes!' The little redhead took his hand and was whisked away where others were dancing.

Curly Joe was back at the table a couple of minutes later, holding a glass of cheap wine. He glanced about, noticing first Amalie's absence, then Tomcat's. His smile rapidly turned to anger.

'That goddam runt! She's my girl.'

'She's a dime-a-dozen whore,' Black Elliot remarked, half-amused.

'Or most likely, about five bucks for half an hour,' Irish added.

Curly set the wine glass on the table hard enough to spill some.

'I'm the one bought her the damned drink,' he cursed. 'And Tomcat with that accent so thick you can't make out half of what he says.'

'He's bringing her back now,' Elliot said calmly, though he wished Tomcat had shown more sense. Sure enough, Tomcat was leading the pretty redhead back to their table. She was laughing and breathless as he sat down and pulled her on to his lap.

'Your wine,' Curly said briefly, pushing the glass towards her.

'Oh, my!' Amalie exclaimed, realizing her mistake.

Tomcat kept his left arm around her waist and fished some coins from his jacket pocket with his right hand. He tossed them across the table towards the Mexican.

'Buy yourself some more whiskey, or wine for another girl,' he said cheerfully. 'Me an' Amalie are getting along just fine.'

Elliot saw Curly tense and put a hand on the other man's shoulder.

'We don't want to draw any more attention to ourselves, do we?' He stared Curly Joe down, imposing his will on the other man. Hate flared for a moment in Curly's eyes, but Elliot kept a tight grip on his shoulder until he felt the other man relax. Elliot gave an inward sigh of relief when Curly picked up the coins.

'We'll go dancing again soon, won't we?' Tomcat asked Amalie.

'I gotta get my breath back first,' she said.

Tomcat leaned closer and drew the tip of his tongue from the base of her neck to her hairline. Amalie gasped and gave a little shudder. Elliot started talking to Curly about poker; Curly made the effort to keep talking, but he kept glancing across the table. Tomcat had one arm around Amalie's waist and was cupping her left breast with his free hand. Her wine was ignored as he delicately nibbled the back of her neck, and touched her ear with his lips. Irish steadfastly ignored Amalie's gasps, and went on talking about poker and drinking his liquor. Tomcat had his fingers inside the front of Amalie's dress and was gently kissing the back of her neck. The pale skin felt as soft as peaches to his lips. Her eyes were wide open and she was breathing heavily. Tomcat could feel the excitement in her body as she wriggled on his lap. He took his hand away from her breast and slid it under her voluminous skirts. Her thigh was warm, encased in fine cotton stocking. Amalie drew in a long breath, pressing herself against him as he moved his hand higher.

Curly Joe finished his drink in one go, slapping the glass down hard on the table. He rose swiftly, his dark eyes burning.

'*Adios.* I see you tomorrow,' he snapped, striding away from the table.

Tomcat's green eyes glittered. 'He looked madder'n a blind dog in a butcher's shop.'

Amalie giggled and drank her wine. 'Can't let this go to waste, as he was so nice as to buy it for me.'

'You don't want to be doing that too often,' Elliot warned Tomcat. 'Folks like him hold grudges.'

Tomcat grinned. 'He's jealous 'cause he cain't dance.' He slid his hand to the top of Amalie's stocking and touched the soft flesh there. She set down her half-drained glass and turned to kiss him. Tomcat kissed her hard in return, relishing the contact of their bodies. When they broke off the kiss, he asked:

'Is there anyplace quieter we can go?'

As Tomcat well knew, the girls were supposed to stay in the saloon and encourage men to keep buying them drinks. Tomcat saw no point in wasting money on the drinks if he could entice a girl to leave.

Amalie nodded. 'My room upstairs.' She was reluctant to get off his lap, but once Tomcat had slid her from his lap to the floor, she took his hand and hurried him towards the staircase.

Irish and Black Elliot watched them leave. Elliot was the first to speak.

'For sure she'll forget to ask him to pay.'

Irish nodded. 'They usually do.'

Hugh was in good spirits as he prepared to go out that evening. Darrow had used his appointment as best man to insist that the bachelor night took place well in advance of the actual wedding.

'I've seen what you look like the day after you've been drinking,' he drawled. 'Minnie might take to having second thoughts about saying 'I do' to the in sickness and in health part, iffen you're standing next to her, looking like you want Turnage to pack you in a pine box and have done.'

'I would have liked to have asked him to be an usher,' Hugh said as he tied his boots. 'But it didn't seem right to have the town undertaker looming up at the church door, asking 'Bride or groom?'

Darrow laughed and picked up his jacket.

'Let's go get it over with.'

The Empty Lode saloon was busy for Hugh's bachelor night. The more respectable people invited, such as Justice Robinson ('We've never liked one other, but he'll be offended if I don't ask!' Hugh had said to Darrow earlier), would only stay for a drink or two before finding a polite reason to leave early. There were plenty of others who were willing to drink to their friend's future happiness. Hugh's arrival was greeted with cheers, making him stand straighter than usual. He made his way to the bar, nodding to a few particular friends, and produced two fifty-dollar notes. These he handed with great flourish to Nation, the saloon owner.

'The first round is on me,' he declared. Looking

around, he noticed a large man with long blond hair and a goatee, sitting at a table in the corner with a smaller friend dressed in brown. 'You're included too, strangers,' Hugh said expansively. 'I'm getting married in six days.'

'Congratulations,' said the large man. The rumble of his deep voice was hard to hear in the noisy room. His wiry, bright-eyed companion raised his beer glass as a gesture of thanks.

'Here's your first, Hugh.' Nation put a generous tumbler of fine whiskey in front of the Englishman. Hugh picked up the glass and tipped back the contents with practised ease. As the glass was being refilled, Hugh found Josh Turnage standing next to him. Since their last meeting, the undertaker had grown a fine moustache, waxed and curled at the ends.

'Good God, Josh. You look like something out of a cheap melodrama!' Hugh exclaimed.

The lean undertaker's eyes glittered as he leaned closer. 'Excellent,' he hissed.

Hugh swallowed rapidly, and reached for his next whiskey.

Turnage laughed, which was hardly more reassuring.

'I wanted to look the part for the squire in *Mary Bates – or A Maid's Dishonour*, the cheap melodrama that the Amateur Players Society are putting on at the Civic Theater next month,' Turnage explained, twirling the end of his moustache with his finger.

'I never thought of you as the theatrical sort,' Hugh said.

'A lonely undertaker's got to find something to do

in the evenings,' Turnage answered. 'I want to try and meet some women who are still breathing. Trouble is, most of them aren't too keen on a husband that's got dead folk in the shop downstairs.'

'I see your point,' Hugh answered sincerely. He patted his lean friend on the shoulder. 'Have another drink.'

The evening passed quickly, at least from Hugh's point of view. He played poker for a while, which kept him from getting drunk as quickly as he might otherwise have done. When he was fifty dollars up, he took the money to the bar and announced another round of drinks. John Cage started a chorus of 'For He's a Jolly Good Fellow,' which had Hugh flushing with pleasure as he leaned rather heavily against the bar. Another large whiskey went down quickly, before Darrow had time to propose a toast. A stern look to the barman from the sheriff, who had been limiting his own intake in the certain knowledge that he would be putting his deputy to bed at the end of the evening, made sure that the next drink that went into Hugh's glass was smaller.

By closing time, Hugh was still in his chair, if not on his feet.

'I shall not be getting inebriated like this once I am married,' he said solemnly.

Darrow was sitting on one side, Whiskers on the other. Cage, Richard and Turnage faced them across the large circular table. Richard spoke.

'Cheer up, old chap. There will always be occashuns when getting drunk is acceptable.' After one complaint about the vile quality of American whiskey, Richard had joined in with the rest.

'Not when one is married to a woman like Minnie,' Hugh declared.

'Hear, hear!' Cage applauded.

Hugh pushed his chair back and stood up, putting one hand on the table to balance himself.

'The Good Book says that a virtuous woman is worth a price beyond rubies, or something like that.' Hugh lifted his hand to point briefly at Richard, swayed, and grabbed the table again. 'You have brought rubies, and pearls, and diamonds . . . and emeralds . . . and . . .'

'Sapphires?' Turnage suggested.

'Sapphires!' Hugh said triumphantly. 'The jewellery which is the heritage of my proud house, the house of Keating of Market Hanborough, many times honoured by its sons on the field of battle, is to be the dowry for my wife. And you know what?' He looked at them blankly for a moment.

'For sure, we're just dying to find out,' Darrow drawled.

Hugh straightened up in an attempt at dignity. 'Minnie is worth more than all the necklaces, rings, bracelets and tiara-ra-ras in that bloody great safe. And I'm damned if I know why she's marrying me.' Keeping hold of the table with one hand, he raised his glass with the other. 'To Minnie!'

The toast was echoed around the room, most quietly by the two men sitting in the corner. Tomcat Billy leaned closer to Irish; his green eyes alight.

'Did you hear that? There's a sure-nuff' fortune in jewellery in this here town.'

'Sure an' they must be exaggerating,' Irish answered. 'Who would be after owning baubles like that in a town like this?'

'Our good landlady's been rattling on about the wedding of the English lord every time we've done seen her,' Tomcat reminded him. He instinctively kept his voice low, even though the table where the Englishman was sitting was rowdy enough to cover his words. 'That's him yonder, and he's just been yapping 'bout the jewellery of his proud house. I reckon the other Limey toted it here, and it's in one safe, probably where the tall Brit is staying.'

Irish smiled slowly. 'I like the idea of taking jewellery off an English nob.'

'We'll tell Black Elliot in the morning,' Tomcat decided. He drained his drink 'Let's slip out now, while they're still keeping the place lively. I'll go first an' wait till the tall Brit leaves. I'll follow him back and find out where-at he's staying.'

Irish nodded; he knew how silently Tomcat could move in his moccasins.

The thief's departure was unnoticed by the local sheriff. He was busy making his deputy drink some water, before attempting to get him home.

Early the next morning, Tomcat Billy sent a note to Black Elliot's hotel room to say he wanted a meeting there at ten. Tomcat didn't possess such a thing as writing paper, but solved his problem by swiftly unpinning the newest notice from the board outside the sheriff's office and carrying the paper to the drugstore on the other side of the street, where Irish

41

was having coffee. The note was written on the back of the wanted notice in carefully formed capitals, using a stub pencil. Tomcat folded the paper to hide both his message, and the printed matter, then wrote Black Elliot's room number on it. He put the pencil back in his jacket pocket with a sigh of relief. Irish held out a large hand.

'I'll be finding some kid to take it while you get a drink,' he offered.

'All right.' Tomcat turned to study the list of sodas and iced drinks.

Irish put the money for his own drink on the counter and left the cool drugstore. All the stores and businesses had awnings to provide shade from the summer sun but the heat was still uncomfortable, even for Irish, who felt the cold easily. He loosened the neck of his flannel shirt, and looked about. A boy of about seven was playing with a ginger cat on a bench in front of the sheriff's office, across the street. Irish waited for a wagon loaded with bolts of fabric to pass, then crossed the street.

'Could you be doing a job for me, boy?' he asked. 'I'll give you a quarter to take this note to this room in Pinder's Hotel.'

'Sure thing, sir,' the boy said eagerly. He took the note and the quarter and set off at a run.

Irish smiled; a dime would have been plenty, but he liked giving money to children. His pa had been killed down the mines when he was six, and there had been many times when he had longed for a dime to himself. Irish wandered back to the relative cool of the drugstore to pass the time.

# CHAPTER FOUR

At ten, Tomcat and Irish entered Pinder's Hotel separately and inconspicuously. Irish waited until the desk clerk was busy, then simply walked in, crossed the lobby without catching anyone's eye, and went up the stairs with the air of a man who had every right to be there. Tomcat picked a moment when the stableyard at the back was empty and jogged across to the stable adjoining the main building. Although he was wiry, he was an expert climber and stronger than he looked. Tomcat took a quick run and jumped half-way up the stable wall. By using the door lintel and the angle of the walls, he was on the flat stable roof with no apparent effort. From there it was a long step on to Black Elliot's window-ledge and he was in through the open window. The whole manoeuvre had taken scant seconds.

'*Madre de Dios*!' Curly Joe exclaimed theatrically as Tomcat made his entrance. 'You are the biggest cat I ever saw.'

Tomcat smiled. 'Why, Curly, that's for-sure the nicest thing you ever done said to me.'

Black Elliot's room was comfortably furnished with

a double bed, walnut wardrobe and chest of drawers. A three-part screen covered in Chinese silk partially hid the washstand, where his shaving kit was neatly laid out. Elliot was sitting in an armchair, Curly Joe had taken the chair by a small, maple-veneered writing-desk. Irish was sitting on the bed, his large feet planted on the rug beside it.

'Did you ask us to meet you here just so as you could make a fine entrance?' Black Elliot asked Tomcat. He stood up and walked towards the smaller man.

Tomcat held his ground; his grin was wider than ever. 'I got some interesting news for you-all.'

'It had better be very interesting,' Elliot returned. 'We're taking a risk, getting together.'

Tomcat glanced at Irish before speaking to Elliot again.

' 'Member that fancy wedding we're fixin' to use as diversion for the bank job? Well, the lucky husband and his friends was celebrating the occasion in the Empty Lode last night; they was even good enough to buy us a drink or two. That husband is a for-real English lord. And his brother done brought a whole safe-full of jewellery to this here town, for this lord's wife. It's their family inheritance and it's in this hotel!'

Elliot got out his harmonica and blew a few notes, looking at Tomcat. The small man was genuinely excited, and Elliot felt a sudden thrill.

'What sort of jewellery?' he demanded.

'They was talking 'bout emeralds and sapphires and diamonds. The Englishman sure was drunk; he kep' talking about his wife being like a queen.'

'He said there were necklaces, bracelets and rings in the safe,' Irish added.

Elliot felt something almost like the bellyache he had got from eating bad pork one time. But there was an exhilaration in this. He kept his face calm and blew on the harmonica as the thoughts raced around his mind. Jewellery was harder to dispose of than cash, but he had contacts in Chicago. He was the only one of the four who could sell on the jewellery for anything like its true value. He could skim, say, a tenth off the total, then openly divide the remainder amongst the four of them. Elliot was a realistic man. If Curly thought he was being cheated, then Elliot was likely to find a knife in his back before long. Better not to be too greedy. And wouldn't it be one in the eye for that Southern sheriff!

'We can't wait until the wedding,' Elliot decided. 'The jewellery might get moved to a bank vault before then.'

'But the wedding's still our best chance of acting while the town's quiet, *amigo*,' Joe protested.

'The hotel don't have armed guards,' Tomcat pointed out. He was sitting on the windowsill, enjoying the sunshine. 'The bank sure does.'

Curly Joe made a sound of disgust. 'We have dealt with bank guards before.'

'There's surely no point doing so iffen we don't have to,' Black Elliot drawled. 'Banks expect to be robbed, hotels don't.' He put the harmonica to his mouth and breathed a few notes as he thought. The essential plan came quickly. 'Remember how we cleared the bank in Woodville?'

Tomcat did. 'I set a small smoke fire under the floor. When the folks inside smelled smoke coming up through the boards, they all lit out like someone had tied firecrackers to their asses, and we snuck in the back. It was a real whirl-me-round!' He chuckled at the memory.

Elliot nodded. 'We'll do that here. Now that safe's in reception, against a wall. The parlour's on the other side of the wall. Tomcat, you set the smoke under the parlour, close to that wall. Curly, you'll be in there. You get to yelling 'fire' and hurry folks out. Me and Irish will be up here, waiting. Just as soon as everyone's out, I'll blow the safe. Irish will be watching out for me.'

Irish nodded, thinking the plan through slowly. Curly Joe got up and went to inspect himself in the mirror. Tomcat glanced down out of the window he was sitting at.

'We'll need to high-tail out of town real fast,' he said.

Elliot nodded. 'We'll time it just afore the Laramie train leaves. We can slip on the train while all the fuss about the fire is going on at the hotel.' He frowned and played a few bars of 'Garry Owen' before speaking again. 'Two stay in Laramie with the goods, two of us come back on the next train before we're missed, and collect the horses.'

Irish nodded. 'I like that plan. When will we be after doing it?'

'I'll get the dynamite in Laramie today,' Black Elliot said. He took a gold watch from the pocket of his fancy waistcoat and checked the time. 'We'll do it mid-morning tomorrow; the hotel's quiet then.' The others gave their agreement.

Tomcat climbed through the open window on to the ledge, paused a moment, then jumped out and down on to the roof of the stable. He landed lightly, then bent down and swung himself to the ground in one fluid movement. He was out of sight in less than a minute. Curly Joe made a noise somewhere between disgust and admiration.

'He'll run out of lives and break his fool neck, one day.'

'Maybe so,' Irish said absently. 'But *he* won't get buried in this town's boneyard.'

'What do you mean?' Elliot asked sharply, his superstitious fears aroused.

Irish blinked suddenly, and rose. 'Sure an' I was just dreaming,' he said defensively. 'I'll be seeing you tomorrow,' he added, and left the room abruptly.

Curly Joe snorted. 'Don't pay him no nevermind.' He checked the set of his bandanna in the mirror, and left too, leaving Black Elliot feeling uncommonly cold.

Hugh's spirits rose as he approached the carnival with Minnie, Darrow, Richard and Louisa. This time the two lawmen were off-duty and free to enjoy themselves.

'What happened to that fellow you arrested for rigging his game?' Richard asked. He moved sideways to let an excited young child rush past.

'Archer was let out on bail this morning,' Hugh

told him. 'He'll be tried Thursday next.'

'None of these people can be trusted,' Richard grumbled. 'I don't know why I let you talk me into coming here, Hugh.'

'Don't be such an old stick,' Louisa told him. 'We're on holiday. The children are happy with Nanny and we can do whatever we like. Why, I could turn a cartwheel right now, and none of the grandmothers back home would know unless you were foolish enough to tell them.'

Richard was completely floored by his wife's answer. Minnie gasped and then clamped her mouth shut. Hugh was turning red in his efforts not to laugh. Darrow saved the situation by gracefully guiding them in the direction of a nearby stall.

It was a shooting gallery, with playing cards as targets. Points were scored according to the card hit.

'Come along, come along!' the carnie bellowed. He pointed at Richard. 'Show the lovely ladies your skill. Win them a prize; the best prizes for the best shots! You look like an excellent shot to me, sir. Only a dime a try. Five shots a go.'

Nettled by Louisa's remark, Richard handed over a dime and took hold of the light rifle fixed loosely to the stand. His first shot failed to hit any card at all.

'The sights on this are terrible,' he complained, before trying again.

Richard eventually scored enough points to be able to choose one of the better range of prizes, and settled for a cut-glass butter dish, which he held with some pride. Louisa insisted on having a go, to the stallholder's surprise. He was even more surprised when she won herself a bracelet of green glass beads. As Louisa had been shooting regularly since the age of twelve, her opinion was that she would have done better if she had had a shotgun and a moving target. Hugh had a go, and annoyed his brother intensely by potting all four aces, and then the ace of spades again. The disgruntled stallholder rewarded him with a large wax-headed doll wearing a frilly dress, which Hugh promptly passed to Minnie. Hugh looked at Darrow expectantly. The sheriff stared coolly back.

'Why should I waste a dime in order to win some tasteless knick-knack?' he drawled.

'So that you can donate it to the next church tombola and pretend to have a heart,' Hugh shot back.

Darrow pretended not to have heard, and picked up one of the light rifles. He studied the range of prizes, disdain clear in his face at the array of painted plaster and cheap glass items. In his opinion, the least offensive gewgaw he could win was the glass ashtray. Having calculated the score he needed to win it, the sheriff carefully aimed and fired his five shots. Each hit home close to the centre of the card. The last one was dead centre of the ace of hearts.

'Oh, good shot,' Richard said generously.

Darrow wasn't pleased with himself. 'I was aiming for the king.'

'And what are you thinking of this?' Irish showed Tomcat a photograph of himself that he'd had taken the day before, after a visit to the bathhouse and barbershop. They were strolling down the busy sidewalk on Main Street, amongst the shoppers, delivery men and idlers. Irish was carrying a bundle wrapped in an old, greyish towel under his left arm. Tomcat studied the picture for a moment.

'Why you look as smart as a pup with a new collar,' he answered. 'I might get me a picture done and send it to the folks back home.'

Their conversation ended as Tomcat Billy and Irish stopped on the sidewalk outside Pinder's Hotel. The hitching rails were quite full, as the hotel was next door to the Freight Car saloon. Tomcat looked around, taking advantage of Irish's bulk to hide him, and slipped under the hitching rail on to the street. Amongst the closely tied horses, it was easy for him to quickly duck out of sight and wriggle under the sidewalk. The bundle Irish had been carrying dropped to the ground just within arm's reach. Tomcat seized it and pulled it under with him.

Shafts of gilded sunlight struck down into the dark under the boards through gaps where some had warped. Tomcat shoved the bundle further in, under the hotel itself, and wriggled after it. Leaves, paper, bottles and even a battered wooden crate that had once held whiskey bottles had drifted in under the hotel. Tomcat felt as if he were in some secret world, his face a few inches from the earth while footsteps thudded overhead. His sharp ears caught the sound of a mouse skittering away through the debris. He wriggled forward, smelling the dryness of the earth. Even with pulling and shoving the bundle along, it took less than a minute for him to reach the right spot. Tomcat was listening to the muffled voices above, when he heard something else.

A buzzing rattle, no more than a few feet away to his left. Tomcat almost screamed but clamped his teeth together so hard he bit his lip. He screwed his eyes closed and dug his hands into the soil, clinging to the earth in order not to panic. Tomcat forced himself to breathe evenly, no matter how fast his heart raced. The rattle sounded again and Tomcat shivered in spite of the sweat forming on his face. There was a white scar on his right arm where he had been bitten by a rattlesnake two years earlier. The agony, shakes, vomiting and sheer terror of expecting to die, poured back into Tomcat Billy's mind.

Very slowly, he turned to look. The diamondback was partially coiled, with a foot of head and neck, and the end of its tail, raised. It shook its tail again, producing the characteristic buzz. Tomcat took a deep breath and forced himself to let it out slowly. The diamondback could only strike to a maximum distance of about half its own length. Tomcat estimated that he was three feet beyond its current range. He wanted to move, to scuttle backwards away from the danger. Instead he glanced about. The whiskey bottle box he had crawled past was near his feet. Moving slowly, Tomcat wriggled backwards until he could catch the broken box between his feet. He curled himself, holding the box between his feet, until he could reach the box with one hand and bring it up to his face. The diamondback shook its rattle again and coiled itself a little tighter. Tomcat closed his eyes a moment; his heart seemed to pound even louder.

Tomcat opened his eyes again and slowly turned the box so that the open side faced the snake. He shuffled forward a little, the box held in front of himself. Digging his toes into the ground, Tomcat pushed forward fast, thrusting the box over the snake as it sprang in reaction to his sudden move. Tomcat heard its head hit the inside of the box, a few inches from his ear. He pinned the box against the ground as the rattler battered itself against the inside. Already the cracked wood of the old box was giving way. Terror drove Tomcat's reactions. As he had hoped, a few inches of the rattler's tail were on the outside of the box. Seizing the end of the tail, Tomcat jerked the snake out from under the box, rolling backwards at the same time. He whirled it around horizontally, in the narrow space under the building, and cracked it like a whip, using all the strength he could muster in an awkward position. The snake's head broke off under the force, landing with a soft thump, some feet away. Tomcat threw the body to one side and rolled over to vomit up his breakfast.

He lay on his chest for a few moments, letting the terror seep away. As soon as he felt calmer, Tomcat spat into the dirt and unwrapped the old towel to get at his bundle of damp leaves, green wood, and kindling. Tomcat cleared a space to arrange the kindling, then got a match from the tin in his pocket and struck it on a stone. Once the fire was going, he carefully added the green sticks and piled the leaves on them. A good, thick smoke started to coil up from the crackling mass. Some of it had to be filtering up through the floorboards of the hotel, but a lot was spreading out. Tomcat emerged backwards and stood up between the horses at the hitching rail. He coughed and spat smoky phlegm on to the street. A quick wipe with his handkerchief got the worst of the soot from his face. Tomcat spoke to the horse he was standing beside.

'I'm off to wait by the depot and see the fun.' Giving the horse a quick pat on the shoulder, he slipped out and trotted across the street.

# CHAPTER FIVE

At mid-morning, Pinder's Hotel was quiet. Curly Joe was sitting near a window in the parlour, sipping his third coffee and trying to concentrate on reading Govan's daily newspaper, the *Herald*. There were about half a dozen other people in the parlour. The pretty woman, with two shy, pigtailed daughters, was waiting for a train, judging by the bags stacked beside her. Curly identified a man in a brown suit as a travelling salesman and paid no further attention to him.

Curly turned the page of his paper and scowled into it, wondering what was holding up Tomcat. He was trying to concentrate on an article about the local amateur dramatic society, when he noticed the salesman sit upright in his chair and look around. Curly took a deep breath and could definitely smell smoke in the air now. Elliot's orders had been to let the smoke build up as much as possible, so Curly kept quiet as the other man cautiously sniffed the air and looked for the source of the smell. Another minute passed and the air in the parlour was decidedly acrid.

Curly got up and walked towards the wall separating the parlour from reception. Two chintz-covered armchairs partially screened the far corner of the room. Curly leaned over one and started to cough. A deep red carpet covered most of the floor, but smoke was seeping up between the uncovered floorboards, behind the chairs. Curly got behind the chair and pulled up the corner of the carpet. A grey cloud of thick smoke wafted up past him. Curly coughed and backed away, dropping the carpet. He heard some- one yell 'Fire', and a scream from one of the chil- dren.

'Get out!' Curly yelled, waving his arms. 'Get out, quickly.' His second yell ended in a fit of coughing.

The room was hazy with smoke now. Curly's eyes were watering as he stumbled outside, following the others. He dropped on to one of the benches on the sidewalk, and leaned forward to cough up sooty phlegm, which he spat into the street. Now it was up to Black Elliot to finish the job.

Black Elliot had been waiting at the top of the hotel landing with Irish, just out of sight of the people below, but able to hear what was going on. Irish had stood quietly, like an ox waiting in the yoke, but Elliot had kept fidgeting with the harmonica in the pocket of his smart black coat. When the cry of 'fire' had gone up at last, he had waited a couple of minutes for the people to leave, before taking a look and hurrying down the stairs.

'Wait and keep watch,' he reminded Irish as they reached reception. The air was hazy in here but not unbearable.

Elliot slipped through the open flap of the reception desk and made for the safe. It was a good solid black one, with gold ornamentation. Elliot put down the carpetbag he carried, and tried the safe handle quickly, just in case, but it was locked. He took a single stick of dynamite from beneath his coat and carefully wedged it behind the handle. Elliot lit the cord attached to the dynamite and sprinted across the lobby into the dining room. He waited, hoping like mad that he'd got the fuse-length and the force right. Elliot fought back the urge to go and see whether the cord was still burning. He'd seen one knob-headed fool get blown to pieces, through impatience. The blast, when it came, made him jump.

Black Elliot ran back across the lobby and vaulted over the reception desk. Irish followed into the hall, his gun in his hand. The door of the safe was swinging open, sheets of paper littered the space behind the desk and the chair was shattered. Elliot grabbed the carpetbag and kneeled in front of the safe. A bright, fierce light came into his eyes as he saw the jewellery boxes inside. That scrawny Tomcat had been right! Reaching in with both hands, he shovelled the boxes rapidly into his bag. In less than a minute, he had all the jewellery boxes inside and some bundles of notes. Black Elliot snapped the bag closed and hurried into the dining room, Irish behind him, and cautiously peered through a window in the alley between the hotel and the saloon next door.

No one was in sight, so he unfastened the mosquito screen and quickly jumped out. Irish climbed through more slowly after holstering his Colt. They went to the back of the hotel, and after walking unnoticed behind the saloon and the feed store, reappeared quietly back on Main Street. Elliot walked back down the sidewalk, swinging the carpet-bag and humming a tune. Neither man said anything as they strolled towards the railroad depot.

Deputy Pacey was at the leather-topped desk in the sheriff's office, reading old logbooks. The office boasted a couple of chairs, a safe, a filing cabinet with an old hat of Hugh's on top, a rack of shotguns and rifles and a row of coat pegs. There were two home-made shelves which held Darrow's law books, a battered copy of *Great Expectations*, two dime novels, a half-empty pack of coffee and other odds and ends. On the wall behind the desk was a calendar that Hugh had talked the owner of the Freight Car saloon into giving him, and to which Darrow turned a blind eye. By the door at the back of the room, which led to the cells and the stairs, was a noticeboard that held official notices, Wanted posters and a note Hugh had written reminding himself to get his horse shod. The confiscated Wheel of Fortune was a rather incongruous feature in one corner.

Pacey was trying to get an idea of daily life in Govan. Sheriff Darrow's handwriting was even, and his reports were concisely written and formal. Hugh's handwriting was an elegant, if rather illegible copperplate, and the reports often contained last-minute additions. They also showed a tendency towards recording gossip, which gave the new deputy fresh opinions about some of the people he'd met since arriving in town. Pacey put his feet up on the desk, and was engrossed in a fascinating account of a fight at Amy Vialla's brothel, when the screen door crashed open.

'Sheriff!' The newcomer stopped, stared at Pacey, and looked puzzled.

Pacey hurriedly removed his feet from the desk. 'Deputy Pacey,' he announced, showing his badge. 'What is it?' he asked impatiently.

'There's a fire down at Pinder's Hotel,' the man said, waving his arm in the general direction of the hotel.

Pacey bounced to his feet. 'Go to the carnival and find the sheriff; let him know.'

'Yessir!' The man shot out again, banging the screen door behind him.

Pacey slammed the report book shut and pushed it back into its place on the shelves. Grabbing his hat, he left the office at a run.

Elliot slowed down as he approached the railroad depot: something was wrong. Only Tomcat was in sight, walking along the metal rail as a child might, to try his balance. Tomcat spun on one toe, then jumped off the track and ambled to meet Black Elliot.

'Where's Curly?' Elliot asked. His voice was quiet but the tone was dangerous.

'The train ain't coming. Not for another two hours,' Tomcat drawled. 'They done run out of water at Rawlins. Tanks there sprung a leak.' He didn't seem unduly upset by the delay.

Elliot quelled the impulse to hit him. Didn't the fool realize how much had depended on the timing of the train? For a moment, Elliot came close to panic; he'd counted on this train running as usual. Now he needed to alter his plans, and quickly. He realized he was being watching steadily by those green eyes, waiting to see what he would do next.

'So where-at's Curly?' Elliot repeated.

'Figgered it weren't so smart for us to be standing round together longer'n necessary,' Tomcat answered. 'Curly's in the Freight Car. You totin' the goods in that there bag?'

'Yeah,' Elliot answered, thinking frantically. He looked across to the Hotel, less than fifty feet away from the depot. In the time it had taken him to walk part-way up Main Street and back, a bucket-chain had been formed from volunteers. There was still some smoke wafting from the open door, but the trouble seemed to be under control. A tall young man was racing along the sidewalk. He reached the hotel and stopped, demanding to know who was in charge. Elliot and Tomcat could overhear the excited conversation.

'Is anyone still inside?' the tall man asked, peering towards the open doors.

'Place got emptied straight away, Deputy,' Pinder replied. He ran his fingers through his dishevelled hair. 'There was a lot of smoke, then some almighty explosion.'

'I'm going to take a look.' The tall deputy covered his mouth with a handkerchief, and disappeared inside the smoky building.

Elliot made a decision. 'We'll meet at the White Buffalo. You an' Irish go together; I'll get Curly.'

Tomcat nodded. 'I sure need a drink.' He moved off, his thoughts turning to a quick dance with Amalie.

Elliot hefted his carpet bag and went to look for Curly Joe.

At the carnival, Richard had salvaged some pride by getting a better score than Hugh by throwing hard wooden balls at plates. He took his prize of a vase and showed it to his wife.

'Should we give it to Cook for Christmas?' he suggested.

Louisa looked at the vase and shook her head. 'Please don't. Good cooks are so hard to find.'

The carnival party had reached the Tent of Wonders, at the end of the first aisle of booths. A paunchy man with oil-slicked hair and an eye-dazzling checked jacket was standing on a low platform by the entrance, rattling off a list of the exhibits to be seen within. Melodramatic paintings on canvas sheets stood in front of the tent to lure the customers. One showed a picture of a giant turtle, with the legend 'Killer of the Sea' in florid letters. Another picture invited folk to see 'The Grave Robber'. It was depicted in a cemetery, with bones scattered around.

'Why, that's nothing but an armadillo,' Richard remarked contemptuously. 'You remember that stuffed one Uncle Merlin brought back?' he asked his brother.

'You propped it over the nursery door, but it fell on Nanny, instead of me. You couldn't sit down for two days after she beat you for it,' Hugh answered, a trifle smugly.

Louisa caught Minnie's eye, and they both smothered laughter.

Darrow interrupted the brewing argument. 'Are we going to waste our money on this collection of fakes and freaks or not?' he asked.

'I want to see the three-legged man, I won't believe . . .' Louisa was interrupted by someone calling the sheriff's name.

'What is it?' Darrow was instantly alert.

A man stopped in front of them, gasping for breath. He took off his hat and fanned himself with it.

'There's . . . there's been a fire at Pinder's Hotel. New deputy sent me to fetch you.'

'My new riding habit!' Louisa exclaimed. She hitched up her skirts and broke into a run.

Darrow and the others followed her, dodging through the crowds enjoying the carnival. The sheriff was trying to find someone with a horse, and as they approached the river, he was relieved to see Josh Turnage on his way back into town after exercising two of his black horses. Darrow yelled the undertaker's name, changing direction towards him. Turnage heard him and dismounted. Only one horse was saddled but both wore bridles. Darrow vaulted on to the saddled horse and took the reins.

'Fire at Pinder's Hotel,' he said by way of explanation, before urging the horse into a gallop. Richard vaulted on to the other horse.

'Wait for me,' Louisa demanded. She held her hand up to her husband. 'Hugh, give me a leg up.' Turnage hung on to the reins near the bit, as Hugh cupped his hands together and strained himself to lift his sister-in-law up behind her husband. As soon as she was ready, Turnage released the reins and stood back to let Richard follow the sheriff. The black horse moved into a smooth canter, carrying its double burden with ease. Hugh noticed Minnie watching Louisa with admiration.

Turnage looked towards the town. 'I can't see any smoke, the fire can't be too bad.'

'I hope not,' Hugh replied. 'But the jewellery should be safe in the safe.' He took Minnie's hand and set off at a jog, followed by Turnage.

They arrived at the hotel to find Richard on the sidewalk outside, berating Sheriff Darrow. Deputy Pacey was standing nearby, watching the scene calmly.

'They've taken the lot! Blown the bloody safe open and taken the whole damned lot!' Richard yelled at Darrow.

Hugh jumped off the sidewalk to talk to Louisa, who was holding the two black horses.

'What's happened?' he asked, astonished to see that she was crying.

Louisa blinked, but when she spoke her voice was firm. 'Someone created a diversion with a small fire to get everyone out of the hotel. Then they blew open the safe and stole all the jewellery.'

'I want this town searched!' Richard yelled, going red in the face.

'I'll search under every bed and in every closet if I have to,' Darrow replied, his face cold.

'If you don't get that jewellery back, I'll see to it that you lose that shiny badge of yours,' Richard went on.

Hugh winced, but Darrow answered quietly: 'I'm an elected officer of the law in this town, and what's more, I could arrest you, if you were fool enough to hit me.'

Richard slowly unclenched his fist. Darrow gave him a moment to calm down before speaking again.

'I'll send a wire to Laramie and ask them to meet the train. There won't be one going to Rawlins until half-past eleven.'

'The Laramie train is late.' Pacey explained about the problem with the water.

Darrow took command of the situation.

'Josh, will you go up to Norman's livery stable and see if anyone's left in the last hour or so? Pacey, you go to Francis's place on Lincoln Street. We'll meet in my office and plan things out.'

Turnage took his horses from Louisa and rode back up Main Street. Pacey set off to the other livery barn at a run, his long legs covering the ground quickly.

'Why didn't you put the jewellery in the bank?' Darrow snapped at Sir Richard.

'Because I was foolish enough to believe that Govan was a law-abiding town where it would be safe in the hotel,' Richard answered.

'If you believe any town is that safe, then you surely are a fool,' Darrow drawled. He continued speaking before Richard could get a word in. 'We're wasting time arguing about what has already happened. We need to make plans to stop them getting away with it.'

Darrow turned to see what else was happening. Hugh was holding Minnie, who was crying against his chest. Louisa was patting her shoulder and trying to comfort her.

'It's not your fault,' she was saying. 'You didn't ask us to bring the jewellery out here.'

Darrow approached. 'Minnie, there is no sense in blaming yourself for the actions of others. To cry is plumb unnecessary.' He spoke calmly and rationally.

Hugh scowled at him. 'Minnie can cry all she wants.'

Minnie lifted her head and looked at the sheriff. His voice had been firm but she could see the sympathy in his eyes. Darrow touched her gently on the arm.

'I suggest you return to your home and rest. I'm afraid that Hugh will be rather busier than he likes in the next few days.' He offered her a handkerchief.

Minnie took the handkerchief and mopped her eyes.

'You're right,' she said, straightening herself 'You need to get to work.'

'May I come and see your home?' Louisa asked kindly.

'If you really want to,' Minnie said uncertainly.

'I do.' Louisa took her arm and smiled at her. 'Come on.' Years of charity work and committee meetings had taught her how to cope with ladies who became upset with much less cause than Minnie. She took the younger woman away, tactfully leaving the men to start work.

# CHAPTER SIX

The door to the sheriff's office closed behind Fisher, Richard's valet. Darrow carefully blotted his notes on the valet's account of what had happened at Pinder's Hotel, and looked up. Hugh was sitting in one chair, nervously shuffling a pack of cards from one hand to the other. Whiskers, the leathery old-timer who ran the Wells, Fargo office was in the other chair, scratching underneath his brindled beard. The sheriff wasn't pleased to see that the old man had followed his usual hot-weather practice of leaving off a shirt, and had appeared with his upper half clad in no more than a faded and patched pink undershirt.

Pacey had washed his hands and face since attending the fire, but his clothes still smelt of smoke. He was standing by the window, glancing out now and again to keep an eye on the world outside. The handsome man was considerably more relaxed than Richard, who kept shifting his weight from one foot to the other as he smoked a thin cigar. The Englishman radiated an air of impatience that set Darrow's nerves on edge, although no one except Hugh would have been able to tell. Turnage was sitting cross-legged on the floor. The contrast between the childlike pose and Turnage's lean face, with its melodramatic villain's moustache was downright unsettling.

Richard moved forward. 'What are you going to do, Sheriff?' he demanded.

Darrow had barely opened his mouth when Pacey spoke up.

'We need someone at the depot to check anyone getting on the trains,' the deputy said. 'We can spell one another between checking the livery stables.'

'I reckon even Hugh had got that much figured out,' Darrow drawled coolly. He stood up and moved out from behind the desk.

'It was those damned carnival people,' Richard insisted, pointing at Darrow with his cigar. 'A load of good-for-nothing, fly-by-nights who won't earn a straightforward, honest living.'

'And who didn't inherit enough that they don't have to,' Turnage remarked to no one in particular. Whiskers gave a snort of amusement.

'I don't think it was the carnival folk,' Hugh objected, sliding the cards into his jacket pocket. 'In books, and melodramas it's always the gypsies and the circus who are shiftless thieves, but most of them aren't like that. I bet it was someone in town.'

'Half those stalls were crooked.' Richard turned to his brother.

Darrow interrupted Richard's next sentence. 'I reckon Hugh's right.'

There was a momentary pause until Hugh gave an exclamation of triumph.

'Hah! You said I was right and you said it in front of witnesses! I'll write it down in my diary so I know how long it is until you say it again.'

'I doubt if you'll get anything right again before the crack of the Apocalypse sounds,' Darrow retorted.

'The Apocalypse wouldn't dare to start while you're around,' Hugh shot back.

'I'll take that as a compliment.'

Richard impatiently broke up the bickering. 'You're supposed to be getting my jewellery back, Sheriff Darrow. I want to hear some plans.'

'The burglary wouldn't have succeeded if there had been more patrols,' Pacey put in. He moved to the centre of the room and faced Darrow. 'You were off gallivanting at the carnival while the jewels were being stolen.'

'I was off-duty,' Darrow answered icily. 'You were on-duty, sitting right here, while the burglary went on just three buildings down the street!' He carried on while he had the advantage. 'Stopping the jewels from leaving Govan, and trying to search the town, will take extra manpower, for sure. Josh, Whiskers, I want to swear you in as special deputies, usual wages.'

Josh Turnage nodded. 'Joe can keep the place running a couple days or so, if I keep an eye on him. John Cage will do any mortuary work necessary. I can help out here.'

'And me.' Richard moved towards the sheriff. 'Not for wages of course. I'll put up a reward of one thousand dollars. That might help flush out some of the rats.'

Darrow looked at the Englishman thoughtfully and shook his head.

'This could be dangerous work. Criminals here carry guns regularly, and they surely do use them. Have you ever shot a man?'

'Certainly not.' Richard looked indignant at the idea. 'England's a civilized country.'

Hugh groaned. 'Ever heard of tact, Richard?'

'What? Oh.' Richard bowed slightly in Darrow's direction. 'My apologies, gentlemen. However, these are my family heirlooms that are missing, and I have a duty to assist in their recovery.'

Darrow knew that he would need all the manpower he could get. Richard was irritating, but he could ride and shoot, and had apparently inherited his brother's share of courage, to go with his own. The offer to work for free appealed to Darrow's practical side, but he could foresee problems.

'If you swear the oath, Richard, you will be an acting deputy of this town,' Darrow said clearly. 'I am the sheriff. You will take orders from me. I may listen to your suggestions, but I do not have to act on them. This is my town.'

Richard opened his mouth to answer, then closed it again while he thought. Darrow kept his dark eyes locked on Richard's. After a few moments of silence, Richard nodded slowly.

'Two generals is one too many,' he said.

'Now let's get to work.' Darrow moved back to his desk. 'I want this town sealed up and searched. We'll be at the station for every train, all departing passengers searched. I'll wire Laramie and let the sheriff there know; he can keep an eye on new arrivals in his town. Then I'll see Justice Robinson about getting the trail to the north of town closed off. Anyone who wants to leave town will have to take the trail to the south and be searched. There'll be someone up in the church belltower, watching for anyone trying to sneak out of town. We'll also have to search almost every building in town.'

'What about the nights?' Deputy Pacey asked. 'It'll be easy enough for anyone to sneak out in the dark.'

'There'll be night patrols,' Darrow announced.

'As well as everything you want us to do in the day?' Hugh objected. He sat upright and pointed at the sheriff. 'You might be as tireless as a steam engine, but I'm human.'

'Complete with all the usual failings,' Darrow answered.

'Hugh's making sense,' Turnage remarked. He uncrossed his legs and stood up without needing to lean on his hands. 'There's only six of us; that's not enough to do all those things.'

'Seven,' Richard said. 'Fisher, my valet, will help. There must be some men we can hire.'

Hugh suddenly spoke. 'I've got an idea.' He leapt to his feet and headed for the door. 'I'll be back in a few minutes.'

Darrow frowned as Hugh left; he didn't trust Hugh's good ideas. He was pleasantly surprised a few minutes later when Mr Davis, Minnie's father, entered the office.

'Hugh told me what had happened, and asked me

to help out,' Mr Davis explained. 'I'll be glad to do what I can.'

'I'm mighty grateful,' the sheriff replied honestly. He knew that Davis had fought and survived through four years of the Civil War, albeit on the other side from himself. Davis would be sensible and reliable, which were qualities Darrow needed in his volunteers.

'I don't want Minnie's wedding day spoilt, iffen I can help it,' Davis said. 'I'll do whatever you need me to, Sheriff.'

'I've run out of badges, but I'll swear you in while we wait for Hugh to get back,' Darrow told him. 'Do you know where he went after speaking to you?'

'He didn't say,' Mr Davis answered.

Darrow got his answer a few minutes later, when Hugh returned with Pete and Edison, two of Govan's habitual drunks. The sheriff stared at all three men with undisguised contempt.

'How do you describe this as a bright idea?' he asked Hugh, waving a hand at the drunks. Whiskers nodded a hello to the two men; Richard sniffed the air cautiously and took a long draw on his cigar. Edison took a deep breath of the smoke and sighed in appreciation.

'I haven't had me a smoke like that since 'sixty-nine,' he said wistfully. 'A man gets to miss the fine things in life.'

'If you help out, I'll buy you a box of cigars,' Hugh promised. He turned to the sheriff. 'Pete and Edison have plenty of time to help with searching buildings.'

Pete scratched his bristles and nodded; Edison

nodded too, slightly out of time. They both stared guilelessly at the sheriff.

Darrow stared back at the pair of them. Pete looked hung-over and faintly ill; Edison looked remarkably bright and his shirt looked like it had been washed sometime in the past week. Darrow wrestled with his dislike of the drunks for a moment, before nodding.

'Are you sure these men are suitable?' Richard demanded, moving forward.

'Not in the slightest,' Darrow answered calmly. 'They are, however, available and willing.'

'They're drunks,' Pacey said flatly. He took his Stetson off and fanned himself slowly with it.

Pete and Edison nodded again, still slightly out of time with one another. Darrow had to resist the momentary urge to nod along with them. He covered himself by taking firm control of the situation.

'Pete can work along of you, Hugh,' Darrow ordered. 'Whiskers, you can take Edison for today. You four start on searching this town: hotels, saloons, boarding houses, livery stables. Don't let anyone say "no" to you.' He looked particularly at Hugh as he finished speaking. Hugh returned the look with a scowl, but refrained from saying anything.

'What about these night patrols?' Pacey asked. He moved closer to the sheriff, challenging his ground.

Darrow refused to be put out by the younger and taller man. He simply stared coolly at him for a moment, then looked away and smiled. He was pleased to see Hugh look nervous.

'I aim to draw up a good, large chart of who will be doing night patrols and when. It will be clearly visible on the wall here. There will be three shifts each night, and we will make no secret of the night patrols.' He paused before continuing: 'However, only one shift will actually go out, and it will last roughly half an hour. If folks see one patrol, they will believe that the others happened also. If a man should be out late at night and does not see a patrol, he will assume that the patrol was in another part of the town. The chances of any person being up all night, or covering sufficient of the town to realize that there is no patrol, is minimal.'

Richard frowned. 'Why, that's . . .'

'Brilliant!' Hugh said, grinning.

Darrow smiled suddenly. 'Why, thank you. Now let's get down to business.'

The White Buffalo was a good place to go unnoticed amid the lunch-time rush. The four outlaws sat around one table, the carpetbag hidden underneath it. Black Elliot could barely pick at his food, but Irish and Tomcat both ate stew with relish, spooning it down in the way of men who aren't always sure of when their next meal will be. Curly Joe ate his ham and eggs with careful good manners, somehow keeping his frilly shirt-cuffs clean. Elliot pushed away his unfinished plateful and looked at his gold pocket-watch.

'We'd best be going in a minute,' he told the others.

Tomcat nodded, and washed down the last of his

stew with a mouthful of beer. He let out a satisfied belch and mopped his mouth with a faded, blue handkerchief.

Black Elliot managed not to wince. 'Give me a couple of quarters each, and I'll go pay,' he said.

A minute or so later, they were on their way down Lincoln Street. Black Elliot walked behind Tomcat and Irish, letting himself be partially hidden behind the big man. Curly followed further behind on the sidewalk, glancing at his reflection in the shop windows. No one took any real notice of them. All went well until they turned right after passing the high school and headed towards the depot.

Tomcat, Irish and Elliot had covered about half the distance across the open ground, when Tomcat stopped suddenly.

'They're searching bags,' he hissed.

Black Elliot moved cautiously so he could see around Irish's bulk. There were about a dozen people at the railroad depot, and after a moment, he recognized the sheriff. The sheriff and a villainous-looking man with a moustache, who seemed familiar from somewhere, were moving methodically along the tracks, searching bags, trucks and even pockets.

'Damn that train being late!' Elliot cursed more loudly than he had intended.

'We can be catching the next one,' Irish suggested placidly.

'That sheriff isn't just gonna search one train,' Elliot answered fiercely, managing to keep his voice down. 'We don't stand a chance of getting the jewels out for days.'

'We don't need to get on the train at the depot,' Tomcat suggested. 'We could hop on at some slow point out in the country.'

Black Elliot shook his head. 'And have to hop off again afore we reach Laramie. The sheriff will have wired the news about these jewels across the whole damned state.'

'He's seen us,' Irish rumbled. 'He's for sure wondering what we're doing.'

Black Elliot thought quickly. 'It's obvious we were heading towards the depot.' He took a quick glance back. Curly was nowhere to be seen; he must have realized something was up when they stopped walking. 'Irish, you get on the train. If he asks, tell the sheriff you need some clothes and they don't stock anything here large enough. Come back this evening.' Elliot nodded at the big man and waved to him.

Irish caught on quickly and began walking away from the others, waving back at them.

'Don't be wasting your money on any fast women now,' Tomcat called after him. 'Spend it on the ones who go slowly.'

Irish laughed and ambled across to the group of people waiting at the depot.

'Let's go,' Elliot muttered. He turned and headed back up Lincoln Street, Tomcat just behind him. Darrow had been busy putting his plans into action. Deputy Pacey and Richard were at the ford, searching everyone leaving Govan by the north-west trail. Richard's valet, Fisher, was in the church tower, watching for anyone who might try and leave town without sticking to the trails. Hugh was in the office, partly to deal with any other tasks, but also to rest, as he would be doing the first night patrol. In spite of the present situation, Darrow had no doubt of Hugh's ability to fall asleep.

The sheriff finished checking a drummer's bag of merchandise and returned it to the short man.

'Thank you for your co-operation, sir.'

His last words were half-drowned by the whistle of the train in the distance. Forgetting the drummer, Darrow turned his attention to the large man approaching the depot. He waved for the Irishman to join himself and Turnage.

'You've heard about the jewellery thefts?' Darrow asked, watching the big man's face.

Irish nodded, his expression mild. 'You surely won't be finding any jewels in my pockets,' he said, holding his arms out without being asked.

Darrow frisked the big man, delving into the pockets of his clothes.

'What do you do?' he asked, removing a dirty handkerchief and a comb from one trouser pocket.

'I'm a labourer, sir,' Irish answered. 'I'm going to Laramie today to get me some new clothes. For sure and I can't be getting Levis in my size in this town.'

Darrow's search was thorough; he felt the lapels of Irish's jacket, and the hem of his trousers, as well as checking the lining of his faded black Stetson.

'All right, you can go,' he said at last, raising his voice to be heard over the approaching train.

'Thank you, sir.' Irish hurried to the depot to buy his ticket.

When the train had departed, leaving the smell of steam and hot oil behind, Darrow said to Turnage:

'That man is a criminal. Keep an eye on him and his companions.'

Turnage raised an eyebrow. 'How can you tell?'

'The way he raised his arms, and moved when I searched him. Why, he's surely been searched by lawmen before; he knows the routine.' Darrow spoke as if teaching a class. 'And his hands haven't done rough work in some time.'

Turnage nodded, quickly picking up the information. 'A labourer who's worn out his working clothes without getting calluses on his hands.'

'I'll get Hugh to check the old Wanted dodgers,' Darrow said. 'See if he can find anything.'

The sheriff looked around at the depot, which was quietening down. Deliveries of goods were being loaded up and driven away. A young man, newly arrived, was waiting rather forlornly by the depot with a battered trunk and a ladies' hatbox.

'There's an hour until the next train arrives,' Darrow said. 'You stay here and search anything trying to leave on the south trail. I'll send Mr Davis to join you, and start searching the hotel.'

'It's going to take a long time to search every building in town,' Turnage remarked, pulling his flat-brimmed hat down a little further to shade his eyes.

'Then the sooner we start, the better.' Darrow strode purposefully away.

# CHAPTER SEVEN

Curly Joe was waiting outside the high school when Black Elliot and Tomcat returned to Lincoln Street. The murmur of voices repeating lessons in unison could be heard from within.

'What are we going to do now? That sheriff, he should go to hell,' Curly snapped.

'He's going to start searching all the buildings in town,' Tomcat informed him, enjoying the other man's irritation.

Curly let out a string of Spanish curses, his voice rising as he went on.

'Quiet it, Curly,' Black Elliot ordered. 'Ain't you got the sense of a seam squirrel?'

Tomcat, standing slightly behind Elliot, was grinning. Curly Joe knew he was doing it on purpose but it still irritated him. He hadn't forgiven that runt for stealing his girl in the saloon, two days back. Curly's dark eyes flashed as he suppressed his anger.

'So what do we do now?' he demanded of Black Elliot. 'We can't spend all day on the streets while the sheriff searches the hotels.'

Two old men were enjoying the sunshine on

benches outside Elton's barbershop, almost opposite the school where Curly and the other two were standing. They were starting to watch the three criminals with more attention than before. The owner of the livery barn next door had brought a fretful chestnut horse outside to groom it in the sunshine.

'That there carpet bag shows up like a hog in a chicken run,' Tomcat added.

Black Elliot had his answer ready. 'We'll go to your boarding-place,' he said, looking at Tomcat. 'And split the jewellery three ways. We'll carry it in pockets, hats, boots, wherever, and carry on like we usually do. The sheriff can search rooms and bags all he likes but, for sure, he won't find anything.'

'What about Irish?' Tomcat asked instantly.

'Soon as he gets back from Laramie, we'll re-divide it four ways,' Elliot promised.

Curly had been thinking through the plan. 'The tiaras; those are too bulky to hide in pockets, *amigo*.' He spoke softly, glancing warily at the men opposite.

Black Elliot's temper rose at the surge of questions and difficulties. His careful plan had gone awry and he didn't like being forced into making quick decisions. He forced himself to think clearly and act like a leader.

'Tomcat can bury them; under a building, where it won't be so obvious. We'll just have to take the risk of them getting found. There'll be plenty left.'

'How long're we going to stay in this here town?' Tomcat asked Elliot. 'I don't care none for kicking my heels in a place where I've worked.'

'We'll wait until the lawman's wedding,' Elliot

decided. 'For sure, half of the lawmen will be there. They won't be able to cover the town properly and we can slip out.'

Curly was getting increasingly impatient. 'We can talk about it later,' he hissed. 'Let's split up and get to Tomcat's place.' Without waiting for an answer, he increased his pace and walked away from the other two, his shiny, high-heeled boots thumping on the wooden sidewalk. Behind him, Tomcat slipped under the hitching rail and jogged silently across the street to make his way back by a different route. Black Elliot hefted the carpet bag and set off after Curly Joe.

Hugh's usual night-time patrols tended to be of the cursory sort, generally enlivened by conversations with drunks and prostitutes. His natural sociability with those who flourished best after dark often served him well in clearing up the occasional disputes. He not only knew the names of all Govan's low-lifes, as did Darrow, he also knew their favourite drinks, and preferred ways of losing money at gambling. Hugh had stopped as many arguments and brawls by standing a round of drinks and chatting to the men involved, as the sheriff had by force of character. Darrow didn't entirely approve of his deputy's methods, but he was willing to tolerate anything that worked.

Tonight, his conversations had been briefer and confined to one subject. Amy Vialla had told her girls to try to search their customers' pockets and to wheedle out any information about the robbery. Even

Queenie, who had only given up her hopes of getting Hugh to marry her when the engagement was announced, had promised to help. Bill had agreed to keep an eye on unfamiliar faces at his gin-palace, a dingy shack that Darrow chose to ignore. Having visited the places of interest to the south of the railroad, Hugh headed back towards the centre of town.

He followed the sidewalk up Main Street, pausing to peer into the window of the sheriff's office. Darrow was at the desk, studying one of his law books in the soft light of an oil-lamp. The sheriff looked tired, but his dark eyes flicked steadily over the pages. Hugh switched his shotgun to his left hand and walked on, passing the shuttered windows of Hinchcliffe's grocery store. Govan was quiet, settling down for the night. A black-and-white cat dashed out from behind the Empty Lode and vanished between the sheriff's office and the grocer's. Hugh trotted down the steps at the end of the sidewalk and walked diagonally over the crossing of Main Street and Cross Street. He glanced up and down the two roads, but there was no one in sight. Turning east into Cross Street, he walked down the side of Turnage's Funeral Parlour. The public entrance to the 'shop', as Josh called it, was on Main Street; a door on Cross Street led up stairs directly to the undertaker's living quarters.

As Hugh passed the side door, he caught a sudden, strong smell of coffee. In a moment, he decided that finishing the rest of his patrol could wait. Hot coffee was far more appealing. He stopped dead and started to turn back. A split second later, a bullet smashed into the wall at head-height, just where he would have been if he hadn't turned. Hugh yelled in surprise and pain as splinters burst out, peppering his neck. He instinctively threw himself forward, landing belly down on the sidewalk. Another bullet crashed into the door above him. Hugh rolled sideways, dropping off the sidewalk to land in the street. Inspired by fear, he ignored the jar of the fall and scrabbled frantically under the sidewalk, dragging his shotgun with him.

Hugh rolled on to his stomach and pointed the shotgun across the street. His breath came in fast gasps as he peered out from under the sidewalk, trying to see his assailant.

'Give yourself up!' he called, more from hope than any realistic expectation.

'Goddam you, limey,' came back the answer.

A figure appeared briefly around the corner of the saloon to fire a shot in Hugh's direction. The muzzle-flash lit up the face of Archer, the carnie who had owned the rigged wheel that Hugh had spotted.

'Surrender, or I'll shoot,' Hugh yelled. It was difficult to sound authoritative when hiding under a sidewalk, but he did his best. As soon as he had spoken, he remembered to roll sideways.

Archer's answer was another shot, ploughing up dirt under the sidewalk almost where Hugh had been lying before. Thinking quickly, Hugh gave a yell of pain. At the same time, he drew his Webley revolver and put it on the ground in front of him. Archer was just too far away for the shotgun to be really effective and besides, Archer was careful to expose as little of himself as possible when he made his shots. Bracing the shotgun on his shoulder, Hugh aimed at the corner of the saloon where Archer was hiding. Closing his eyes, he fired both barrels.

The spray of shot tore into the wooden building, erupting out in a shower of splinters. Hugh heard Archer's cry of surprise and pain as he opened his eyes and snatched up the Webley. Archer had flinched away from the building and was bent over, swearing. Hugh wriggled out from under the sidewalk and aimed his gun at the other man.

'Drop your gun,' he ordered.

'Go to hell!' Bleeding from dozens of splinters, Archer raised his gun.

Hugh fired once and saw Archer knocked backwards. He moved closer, keeping his Webley aimed at the other man until he could see clearly that Archer had dropped his gun. A door opened behind him, golden lamplight falling into the street.

'Hugh, it's me, Josh.' Turnage knew better than to surprise a friend in a gunfight.

'Bring the lamp over here,' Hugh answered. 'I think I've killed him,' he added more quietly.

They approached the fallen man. Hugh's bullet had torn through Archer's chest and blood was pooling beneath him. Archer was gasping for breath, his head turned to one side to let frothy blood flow from his mouth and nose.

'No point sending for Doc Travis,' Turnage remarked, bending down. He passed the lantern to Hugh, took off his jacket and folded it to make a pillow for the dying man.

The lantern-light flickered as Hugh's hand shook.

'I asked him to surrender,' he said quietly, staring at Archer with round, sad eyes.

'I heard you,' Turnage answered. He turned his head to listen to footsteps approaching rapidly from the crossroads. Even in the dark, he recognized Darrow.

Archer was dead in the few seconds it took the sheriff to reach them. Now the shooting had stopped, lights were showing at doors and windows along the street.

'What in hell happened?' Darrow asked, kneeling to look at the body.

Hugh explained, his voice unsteady. Turnage confirmed the sequence of shots as he'd heard them, and Hugh's demands for Archer to surrender.

'If I hadn't stopped to ask you for coffee,' Hugh said, his voice barely above a whisper. He made a sorry picture in the lamplight, with his hair rumpled and blood oozing from the splinters in the back of his neck.

'You go fix some coffee while Josh and I carry Archer into the funeral parlour,' Darrow told Hugh. His voice was as commanding as ever, but Turnage didn't miss the sympathy in his dark eyes. Hugh did as he was told. Darrow and Turnage looked at one another, then bent to pick up the corpse.

'Saves the cost of a trial, I guess,' Turnage remarked.

Darrow gave him a sour look. 'I've lost my share of his fine.'

\*

The sheriff's office was quiet the next morning. Pacey was cleaning the rifles and shotguns while waiting for the next train to arrive. Sheriff Darrow was writing up his report of the attack on Hugh. The peace was broken by the arrival of a visitor. Darrow was not pleased to see the stocky shape of Justice Robinson, a short man with sleekly oiled hair and intense dark eyes in a doughy face. Darrow wiped the nib of his pen and put it in its holder.

'Good morning, Justice,' he said calmly, indicating for Robinson to sit down.

Robinson nodded by way of reply. 'There will be an inquest into the shooting of Archer tomorrow at eleven,' he said. 'Hugh, Josh Turnage and yourself will need to attend.'

Darrow was nettled by Robinson's tone. 'Hugh acted in self-defence. It was surely clear enough.'

'The procedure of the law must still be followed,' Robinson told him. 'And I must have evidence from Hugh before he leaves on his honeymoon. I have rearranged my schedule at some inconvenience to myself in order to have this inquest before Hugh's wedding.'

'Damn inconsiderate of Archer to get himself shot right when you're so busy,' Darrow drawled.

'Levity is hardly appropriate,' Robinson answered sharply. His small dark eyes glittered in a way that reminded Darrow of a rat. 'Have you made any progress yet on finding the jewellery? I've had any number of complaints from travellers who have had their bags searched. It isn't good for business.'

'Either the bags get searched, or the jewellery gets

smuggled out of town,' Darrow said, raising his hand slightly to emphasize his point. 'Which would you rather have?'

'I would rather have the jewellery recovered,' Robinson snapped.

'It isn't your jewellery,' Darrow pointed out.

Robinson banged his fist on the corner of the desk. 'The reputation of this town is at stake, and I care about it, even if you don't, Sheriff Darrow.' The short, stout man glared at the sheriff menacingly. 'You knew there was valuable jewellery in the hotel, but when it was stolen, you were gambling at the carnival.'

'What I do in my time off is my own business,' Darrow retorted. 'The good citizens of this town should be less concerned about what the other good citizens are doing.'

Robinson's face turned red. 'You're not the only man who can wear the sheriff's badge. I could bring a no-confidence vote against you in the council, and install Deputy Pacey, instead.'

Darrow didn't bother looking at the deputy, who had stopped cleaning guns and was openly listening to the argument. The sheriff stood up slowly, looking down at the shorter man.

'You done threatened to take my badge before. I'd argue that the way this town's been booming is proof enough of having good law here. You had better be real sure you can get that vote of no confidence afore you try it.'

Hugh would have been cowed by Darrow's tone, but Robinson glared right back.

'If your blockades affect business now, you can't rely on what you've done in the past,' Robinson answered. He stood up too, leaning forward with his hands on the desk. 'You'd better find some way of solving this, and fast.'

'You want me to search everyone leaving town, search every last building in town, and interrogate everyone in town. What should I do with the other hand?' Darrow enquired sarcastically.

Robinson's face turned red. 'Make damn sure you get yourself and your deputies to Archer's inquest on time,' he spat. Whirling around, Robinson stormed from the office, slamming the screen door. Darrow looked at Pacey.

'You'd better hurry up with cleaning the guns; the next train is due in ten minutes.' He turned away without waiting for an answer and sat down to continue writing his interrupted report.

If he'd had the choice, Black Elliot would have spent the evening quietly in his hotel room, keeping out of sight of the patrolling lawmen and away from any possible trouble. However, Curly Joe wanted lively company and Elliot didn't trust his quick temper, especially when inflamed by drink. He accompanied Curly to the Freight Car saloon, which was next to their hotel, but Curly was restless, complaining the place was too quiet. After just one drink, they left.

'Not the Empty Lode,' Elliot said. 'That's where the lawmen drink. I don't want them seeing our faces and mebbe recalling us sometime later.'

Curly Joe shrugged extravagantly; it was one of the

*latino* gestures he affected.

'So long as there is whiskey and women,' he said.

Their next stop was the White Buffalo saloon. Curly Joe pushed through the swing-doors first, his face bright with anticipation. Fiddle and piano music competed with the din of the customers, drinking, gambling and dancing. The air inside was warm, and hazy with the smoke from tobacco and the oil lamps. The two men started to weave their way between tables to the long bar. Curly glanced across at the dance floor, and stopped dead.

'*Hijo de puta!*' he spat, his face turning ugly.

Black Elliot followed his gaze. About a dozen or so couples were on the dance floor, circling to the lively rhythm of a polka. Elliot soon spotted Tomcat Billy, his arms around the red-haired girl he'd lured away from Curly a couple of days ago. Tomcat danced as well as he climbed things, neatly steering the laughing, breathless saloon girl between the other couples as they whirled around.

'I'll slice his ears off and then see if the women like him so much,' Curly hissed, his hand moving to his knife.

Black Elliot grabbed his arm. 'You want to bring the law down on us?' His voice was quiet but urgent. 'That two-bit whore ain't worth it, dammit!'

Curly glared at him. 'He made me look a fool.'

'You'll look a bigger fool if you bring the law running when you've got enough stuff in your pockets to buy a hundred women like her,' Black Elliot said bluntly. 'Besides, that Irish won't be far away. You try touching Tomcat and he'll rip your arms off.'

'I can deal with both of them,' Curly insisted. He was still watching the dance floor.

The polka had ended. Amalie clung to Tomcat, somewhat dizzy from the pace he'd set. He kept his arms around her, and bent a little to kiss her on the cheek. She smiled, reviving, and pressed her body firmly against his, giving a little wriggle that set her bosom quivering. Tomcat grinned, and kissed her on the throat, before leading her into position for the next dance. Curly spun around and barged his way out of the saloon. Elliot followed, cursing the delayed train which had forced them to stay on in this town.

They passed the rest of the evening in another saloon. Black Elliot managed to soothe Curly's ruffled temper by buying a bottle of top-quality whiskey. He kept the bottle close to himself, and poured the drinks carefully, distracting Curly with talk and the musical turns performing on the low stage at the back of the room. While Curly whistled at the line of dancing girls, Elliot was thinking and planning. He felt a grudging respect for the sheriff's efficiency in sealing off the town. The night patrols had been reported on around town, and all public stables were padlocked after dark. If you needed a horse, you had to find the owner of the stable and get him to open it. It would be possible to overpower one person and make a getaway, but the sound of horses moving after dark was bound to attract attention, as things were. A thousand-dollar reward was enough to make most folks interested in stealthy goings-on.

How many men did the sheriff have available? Not more than half a dozen, surely. If two or three of them could be eliminated, they might be able to get out of this damned town before things got organized again. And if that smart Southern sheriff was one of those eliminated, then so much the better. Elliot half-smiled to himself as he sipped the smooth whiskey. He was beginning to feel good again. While the sheriff was still playing catch-up, he, Black Elliot, would be setting the rules of the game.

# CHAPTER EIGHT

Hugh yawned as he clattered down the steep wooden stairs from the living-quarters of the sheriff's office. He missed the last step and stumbled into the office. Hugh managed to catch his balance just short of landing on his knees, but staggered ungracefully before coming to a halt near the coat-rack.

'Good morning.' Deputy Pacey glanced pointedly at the clock on the wall. 'It is still just about morning,' he added.

Hugh scowled at the taller, younger and more handsome man. 'I was up, God-knows-when, doing the last night patrol with Edison.' He rubbed his hands across his face to try and waken himself. Pacey held up his hands in a gesture of peace, and smiled so charmingly that even Hugh softened a little. The deputy stood, walked around the desk and perched himself on one corner, his long legs swinging.

'You've lived in Govan a few years, haven't you?' he asked.

'Yes.' Hugh answered with a touch of suspicion in his voice.

Pacey smiled again. 'I reckon you're the man to talk to; you're a little more ... worldly than our

91

upright and decent sheriff. A lawman's got to look respectable but . . .'

Hugh knew perfectly well that Darrow had been supplementing his official salary for years by pocketing minor fines that weren't registered in the log book. Something about the look in Pacey's blue eyes suggested that he wasn't talking about money, though.

'He'll tell you not to do it, ignore it if you do, and yell at you if you get into trouble for it,' Hugh responded with a promptness born of experience.

Pacey laughed. 'Sounds like you can help me out. What are the girls at the Velvet Cat like?' Hugh was about to answer when he was interrupted by a boy appearing in the doorway.

'Do you want something?' he asked, trying to remember the boy's name.

The boy hurried across the room to him, glancing once at Deputy Pacey.

'I done found something, sir,' he said, excitement colouring his voice. He thrust a grubby hand into his trouser pocket and brought out something to show. Pacey slid off the desk and leaned closer to look. Hugh picked two small items from the boy's palm and held them up.

'The jet earrings!' he exclaimed delightedly. 'Aunt Anne sent a set of jet jewellery over as a wedding present; earrings, necklace, bracelet and a brooch.'

'You're sure they're from the same set?' Pacey asked.

'I never forget a piece of jewellery,' Hugh answered confidently. 'Where did you find them?' he asked the boy.

'You know them shanties near the river, just by the laundry? There's one been empty since the old man froze to death last winter,' the boy said with rather ghoulish glee.

'I know it,' Hugh replied.

'I heard someone talking inside that shanty,' the boy rattled on. 'An' I went to take a look-see but then I saw them earrings just outside. There's a reward for them, ain't there?' he finished eagerly.

'How long ago?' Pacey asked urgently.

'I come straight here,' the boy answered.

The tall deputy grabbed his grey Stetson from the desk and strode over to the gun-rack on the far side of the room.

'We'll go get them now,' he said, taking down two shotguns, and throwing one to Hugh.

'Is there a reward?' the boy asked again.

'For returning the lot, or information leading to capture of the thieves,' Hugh answered distractedly. Pacey was moving about the room like a whirlwind, grabbing a couple of boxes of shotgun shells from the safe and dumping one on the desk next to Hugh.

'We should send for Darrow,' Hugh protested to Pacey as he stuffed the whole box of shells into the pocket of his brown jacket.

'There's no point in wasting time,' Pacey answered, sliding shells into his shotgun. 'We know where they are; we can get them bottled up.'

Hugh plonked his shotgun on the desk and hauled out his wallet. He handed a five-dollar bill to the delighted boy.

'Run and tell the sheriff what you told us. He's at the railway depot.'

'Yes, sir!' The boy bounced from the sheriff's office and out into the sunshine.

Hugh just had time to buckle on his gunbelt, pick up the shotgun and grab a handful of extra rounds for his Webley before Pacey hustled him out the back of the building and away.

Pacey set off at a fast walk, forcing Hugh to break into a jog to keep up with him. They threaded their way between some of the larger houses on this side of town, before reaching the cluster of lumber and tarpaper shanties that had grown haphazardly by the river. Laundry fluttered on lines hung almost above slop piles. A woman shelling peas on her doorstep, seeing the deputies hurrying past with shotguns, called for her children to come inside. Pacey began to look about uncertainly, and slowed down, looking back at Hugh.

'Are we close to the empty place?'

'You don't know where we're going, but you had to rush off like your trousers were on fire,' Hugh grumbled. 'For all you know, old Clapton's place could have been any of those you just went running up to, with God-only-knows who waiting inside.'

Pacey ignored that, instead gesturing for Hugh to take the lead. Hugh thumbed back the hammers on his shotgun and walked cautiously on. He stopped at the corner of the building and peered around to his left. Pacey was close behind, his gun at the ready too.

'That's it.' Hugh pointed diagonally across the space between shanties.

Pacey stretched up and looked over the other man's head. The shanty Hugh indicated had a window each side of the door; one was boarded up, the other had had the glass cleanly removed by an opportunist. The other windows weren't visible from this angle, but Pacey noticed something else.

'There's some smoke coming from the pipe of the cookstove,' he said quietly.

'Someone's been in and out lately,' Hugh remarked, seeing that the long grass around the door had been trampled recently. 'Let's wait for Darrow to get here.'

Pacey shook his head. 'We can get the drop on them easy. Go straight in through the door and take them by surprise. No scalawag's gonna argue with two men carrying scatterguns.'

'What if it isn't the thieves in there?' Hugh objected.

'Then we apologize nicely. Do you want to get your Minnie's jewellery back or not?'

Hugh quailed under the stern look in Pacey's blue eyes.

'All right. But you can kick the door open.'

Pacey gave him a devilish grin and lifted his shotgun.

'Let's go.'

Together they ran across the narrow piece of open ground, to the front of the shanty. Hugh stopped just beyond the boarded-up window, while Pacey halted in front of the door. Pacey didn't waste time, but delivered a powerful, stamping kick to the door by the latch. The door crashed open and Pacey plunged into the gap, dropping his shotgun to waist height. Hugh was moving after him when a shot blew a chunk of splinters from the wall beside him. More shots echoed around them, coming from somewhere outside.There was no one inside the shanty; the ambushers were hidden among the buildings around it. Hugh heard something crack past his head as he dived towards the safety of the open doorway. Something hit his leg as he threw himself untidily through the door and landed rolling. Bullets flew in through the empty window, almost catching Pacey as he kicked the door shut. Hugh rolled on to his back and sat up, gasping for breath.

'I told you we should be careful!' he exclaimed.

Pacey ignored him, and flattened himself against the wall by the empty window. Another bullet tore through and buried itself in the far wall. Hugh's eye was caught by the shafts of sunlight let in through the holes in that wall: bullet holes. He scrambled to his feet and lunged towards the other deputy.

'That's not safe! The wood's too thin.'

He'd barely spoken when a shot hit the door and punched through it, swinging the door open again with its impact. Hugh felt the bullet tug his jacket, missing him by less than a hand's breadth. The shock made him miss his stride, so he fell against Pacey and knocked both of them to the ground. Another round punched through the wall right where Pacey had been standing.

The two men disentangled themselves and crawled further into the room.

'You got us into this mess,' Hugh said, his soft eyes

round with fear as bullets continued to rip into the room. 'How are you going to get us out?'

Pacey looked around the abandoned shanty. The cookstove was still in place, along with a couple of wooden boxes for chairs and a home-made table. The only other signs of life were a couple of empty whiskey-bottles and a mouldering piece of fabric that might have been a patchwork comforter once. At the back of the room was an open doorway leading into the single bedroom.

'We'll use the table,' he said, starting to crawl towards it. 'Turn the top against the wall; should be thick enough to stop anything shy of a buffalo rifle.'

Hugh crawled reluctantly after him, increasingly aware of pain in his right leg.

'What if they've got a buffalo rifle?'

Pacey shook his head. 'Sounds different. The folks outside are using Winchesters.' As he lectured, he tipped the table over carefully, keeping the top between himself and the front of the shanty. The shooting had stopped for nearly half a minute. Hugh looked fearfully at Pacey.

'Do you think they've given up?' he asked hopefully.

Pacey started to shove the table across the floor. 'You want to stick your head out the door an' see?'

Hugh didn't answer; he grabbed a table leg and pushed. Together they heaved the table over to the front of the shanty and pushed it up against the wall under the glassless window. The two men crouched behind it, breathing heavily from their sudden exertions. Hugh eyed the solid wood of the table top and hoped it would be thick enough. Pacey put his shotgun down and drew his pearl-handled Colt Peacemakers.

'I'll take that quick look-see,' he said, with a reckless smile, and popped his head up. He fired a snap shot and ducked back down again. 'One was sneakin' up on us,' he said, the last words being drowned in the crash and thud of bullets.

Lead pierced the shanty wall and hit the table, but none came through. Hugh flinched but kept calm enough to follow the other man's example and draw his Webley revolver. The shotguns were lethal at close range, but revolvers were better in this situation.

'Did you see any others?' Hugh asked, shifting position slightly to take weight off his right leg.

Pacey shook his head. 'Saw some gunsmoke between those shanties opposite.' He gathered himself, them jumped up, firing with both guns before ducking back again. A bullet tore splinters from the window frame as he dropped, missing his head by inches. Pacey gave a short yelp as the splinters hit his face.

'Idiot!' Hugh said. 'I sent that boy to fetch Darrow. We've just got to hold out until he gets here. There's no point . . .'

He stopped speaking at the sound of a thud from the back of the shanty.

'Someone's sneaked into the bedroom,' Pacey hissed. Blood was trickling down his cheek. 'Go take care of them.' He gave Hugh a push and turned his attention back to the window.

Hugh didn't much care for the idea but went

anyway, revolver in hand. He moved as quietly as he could while keeping bent low. If there had ever been a door between the two rooms of the shanty, it was gone now. Hugh crossed the room slowly and stood by the wall next to the doorway, listening for any movement in the far room. Trying to quieten his breathing, he noticed a new, strong smell. Smoke. Not the gunpowder smoke; he knew that smell better than he liked. Taking a deep breath, Hugh lunged through the doorway, and into the room beyond.

Any furniture had long gone, but some trash and a faded, frayed blanket showed that the place had been used since its owner had died. The blanket was a mass of flames, flames that danced across the wooden floor and leapt up at the worn sacking that served as a curtain to an empty window. Smoke rose in heavy coils, spreading ominously. Hugh exclaimed in surprise and got a lungful of smoke. He backed away, coughing.

'What is it?' Pacey turned away from the window to look. His eyes widened as he saw the smoke creeping through the doorway above Hugh's head.

'It's all burning!' Hugh exclaimed, his face damp with sweat and soot. 'We're going to die here!'

Black Elliot showed a smile of grim satisfaction. His last shot had almost hit the tall deputy when he'd popped up. He was standing in a narrow alley between two shanties, along with Curly Joe. Irish was using another building as cover. As Elliot had guessed, the locals had wisely stayed inside, not wanting to get caught up in a shooting match. He was holding fire for a moment, waiting to see Tomcat again.

'There!' Curly spotted the little thief first.

Tomcat appeared alongside the shanty the lawmen were trapped in, and signalled an 'all well' gesture at them before disappearing.

'If he's done a good job, they'll be coming out soon,' Elliot said. He lowered his Winchester and started to slide more shells into it, only taking his eyes from the shanty for the briefest of moments.

'Won't take that much lead to bring them down,' Curly said contemptuously. 'They walked into that trap as sweet as could be.'

Elliot grinned coldly, his eyes hard.

'Easy enough to expect someone waiting to bush-whack them inside a building. They sure didn't expect Tomcat to trail them and tell us which ways they was coming. We got the jump on them and they're bottled up nice and ready.'

Curly nodded, his spirits rising at the thought of getting a reputation as a lawman killer.

'That was some smart thinking of yourn, *amigo*,' he admitted. He fired another shot into the shanty.

Black Elliot was the first to hear the soft pad of running feet behind them. He whirled, rifle at the ready, to see Tomcat sprinting towards them. His moccasins were almost silent on the hard ground.

'Sheriff's bringing some back-up!' Tomcat gasped. 'Be here any minute.'

Curly grinned. 'We can pick him off besides!'

Elliot shook his head. 'If we go deal with him, we risk the two in there catching us from behind. Even if we downed all the lawmen, someone would see us and word'd go out. Our descriptions would be wired from here to Texas in no time.'

'Dammit; I'm not quitting now!' Curly said.

'I'm pulling out.' Black Elliot broke into a jog. 'Which way's best?' he asked Tomcat, who had followed immediately. He let Tomcat take the lead.

Curly Joe cursed and ran after them. He was angry, but he wasn't angry enough to try taking the sheriff by himself. He might have a better chance later: with, or without Black Elliot's say-so.

Pacey left the window and strode rapidly across the room. He peered carefully through the doorway and saw for himself the flames around the window. There was no chance of getting out the back of the shanty. Pacey retreated fast from the smoke and looked around.

'There's got to be something we can use,' he said, almost to himself.

'There's no water in here,' Hugh replied. 'How else can we put a fire out?'

Pacey suddenly saw something.

'We can smother it!' He holstered his guns and grabbed the old patchwork comforter. It smelt sour and was worn in places but was still fairly heavy.

Hugh holstered his gun too and ran to help. He took one side, sneezing as the dust flew, and straightened out the comforter. With the quilt spread out between them, the two men braved the burning room. The heat hit them solidly, snatching breath that was scarce enough in the smoke-filled room.

Pacey took the lead; he aimed for the remains of the burning blanket.

'Now!' he yelled, coughing.

Hugh's eyes were watering, stinging with the smoke. He released the comforter as he was told, letting it fall. It dropped away from them, landing with a flump on the blaze. The air that blew out from beneath it fanned the remains of the burning curtains. Flames shot to the ceiling. A wave of heat hit Pacey in the face. He cried out and turned away, ducking and trying to cover his face with his hands.

Hugh could barely make out what was happening. The comforter had extinguished most of the blaze on the floor, but the fire was still spreading. Hugh made up his mind quickly; he grabbed Pacey's arm and led the other man back into the relative coolness of the other room. He staggered a couple of paces in and collapsed to his knees, coughing. Pacey was in no better state. His light grey jacket and blue shirt were filthy. Part of his face glowed painfully red where the heat had caught it; the rest was stained with smoke and sweat. He gasped for breath too, shaking with deep coughs.

For nearly a minute, the two of them just coughed, unable to do more. With all the noise of the fire behind him, and Pacey's coughs, Hugh almost didn't notice someone approaching the outer door of the shanty. He glimpsed a shadow, and a figure moving, and struggled to his feet, reaching for his revolver.

'It's Sheriff Darrow.' The familiar voice called out

just before Darrow entered, Turnage behind him.

'You took your time,' Hugh answered, before collapsing again and coughing.

# CHAPTER NINE

It was nearly half an hour before they were back at the sheriff's office. A bucket chain had been organized to put the fire out, and Hugh and Pacey had both had their injuries tended. A bullet had gouged a shallow line across Hugh's leg, which had been efficiently bandaged by one of the women living nearby. Pacey's scorched face had been liberally soused with cold water; his skin was red and sore, but there were no blisters so far. They found Louisa waiting for them in the relative cool of the office. She looked fresh and elegant in a blue dress, in spite of the heat of the day.

'Good Heavens! You look like a pack of chimney-sweeps,' she exclaimed, rising to free a chair for one of the weary men.

Hugh claimed it first, sinking down with a sigh. As the others sat, Darrow stayed on his feet. The workload and worry of the last few days was beginning to show in the lines of strain around his dark eyes. His mouth tasted of the smoke from the burning shanty; he felt sweaty and grubby. Nevertheless, he stayed on his feet and glared at the other men.

'We were just getting by as it was.' Darrow's voice had lost none of its authority. 'Thanks to my damn-fool deputies, we haven't got enough experienced hands to go round, until you two get some rest.'

'It wasn't my idea to go racing off,' Hugh protested, looking venomously at his fellow deputy. 'He wasn't even going to bother letting you know what we were doing.'

'I wouldn't expect you to go and look for danger of your own accord,' Darrow snapped.

'I've got more sense!' Hugh answered hotly. 'I've got a damn good reason not to get myself shot at. I'm going to be married in two days. And then I'm going on a long honeymoon to Europe. I want to live long enough to do all that.'

Memories of his own, long-ago intended trip to Europe, one of the many things lost in the aftermath of the Civil War, sharpened Darrow's temper.

'Your wedding isn't going to be the same if those thieves skip town with your bride's dowry in their pockets.' He stalked over to Hugh, his eyes blazing. 'Get up and go relieve Whiskers from the church tower. He can join me at the railroad depot. Josh, you stay here and clean up some.'

Hugh shrank back into the chair, his eyes wide. 'No.'

Darrow reached for his arm, to pull him from the chair, but suddenly found Louisa at his side.

'I'll go and keep watch from the church tower,' she said firmly, looking him in the eyes. 'I'll be perfectly safe up there, and I'll take my hunting rifle in case I see anything.'

Darrow's first instinct was to refuse. He began to straighten and felt the ache of tiredness in his back.

'Very well.' A hint of smile softened his face. 'I was taught it was bad manners to refuse a lady when she asked for something.'

'It's only common sense to accept help when you need it,' Louisa answered.

Darrow noticed that her voice was softer than her words. He stalled his comment about a shortage of common sense in his deputies and turned his attention to practical matters as Louisa left.

'You-all wash up while I go see Appleton at the depot,' he told the others. He rubbed his face, finding a sore patch where a spark had landed. 'I'll send someone to bring back Mr Davis and Pete to take over at the depot for an hour. Fix yourselves some coffee and get something from Mrs Irvine's, or someplace. We'll talk when we've eaten.'

Pacey and Turnage headed for the door at the back of the office and vanished upstairs. Darrow looked expectantly at Hugh, waiting for him to do the same.

'You work yourself like a machine, sometimes,' Hugh remarked quietly. 'But you're not, and neither are we.' He heaved himself to his feet, and staggered slightly.

Darrow automatically put out a hand to steady him.

'Thanks.' Hugh's eye fell on the sheriff's crescent-and-star badge, pinned to the lapel of Darrow's black jacket. It was dull with soot from the fire. 'Better clean that before you go out,' he said. 'Town should be glad to see you wearing that badge.'

Darrow didn't miss the slight emphasis on 'you'. For once, he did exactly as his friend suggested, and without argument. When he left the sheriff's office a minute later, his badge glittered in the sunlight.

In the meantime, the four outlaws had gathered again in the Empty Lode saloon. The place was busy with the lunchtime crowd and noisy with conversation and the jangle of the piano. Black Elliot ordered four beers and paid for them himself. Now was not the time for rotgut-fuelled arguments.

'Do you know if we downed either of them?' Irish asked, dropping his voice to a low rumble.

Tomcat knocked back half his beer in one go. 'I don't cotton none to this business of taking on lawmen with lead. Killing folks ain't my business.'

Curly gave a contemptuous snort.

'Then I bet you're happy we didn't stay to try and take the sheriff too.' He turned his attention to the half-caste, Elliot. 'We didn't finish off that job. What are we going to do now? Sit around and hardwinter like old men?'

'Iffen we'd stayed we could have gotten caught between the sheriff and his man, and the deputies when they came out of the shanty,' Elliot told him.

'*If* they came out,' Curly retorted. He took a swig of his beer before resuming his attack. 'We could have got this over and done, *amigo*, and been on our way out of this damned town.'

There was truth in Curly's accusations, and Black Elliot knew it. The chances were that at least one of the deputies had been injured in the ambush. With quick, quiet Tomcat as scout, they could have set an ambush for the sheriff and most likely taken out him and the undertaker. Elliot suppressed a shudder; he had a superstitious dread of undertakers and coffins. The idea of tangling with an undertaker in a fight gave him the chills. However, it wasn't just that fear that had made him decide to retreat.

'Gunfights in the middle of towns have witnesses,' Elliot said. He stared at each man in turn. 'There could be folks watching we never saw. And unless we could be certain sure the lawmen were dead when we left, they'd be witnesses too. You want your face on a Wanted dodger for killing lawmen?'

Irish shook his head vigorously. 'I don't want that kind of trouble.' He pushed his long, fair hair back off his face.

'Nor me,' Tomcat added, his green eyes bright and alert. 'Let's get the hosses and head for tall timber now, whiles the lawmen are busy working out what hit them.'

'There's gotta be someplace that ain't being watched right now,' Curly agreed.

For a moment, Black Elliot thought of taking up Tomcat's suggestion. They could probably get a good head-start on any pursuit and he was getting sick of this damned town. His caution won out, though.

'Same thing goes. We couldn't skip town without someone seeing us and we can't get the horses night-time without risking a fuss. Even if we did, soon as our horses were noticed missing, the livery owners could tell the lawmen whose horses had gone.' This last point only occurred to Elliot as he spoke.

He saw the dismay in the faces of the other men; he was losing their confidence and fast. Elliot reached into his jacket pocket for his harmonica, and felt the stones and metal hidden there.

'We could steal someone else's horses,' Curly suggested, carefully keeping his voice low.

Elliot was thinking fast.

'They can't search every last place you could hide something, especially at busy times, like when the train arrives. We can take turns riding out, different times, taking the bedsprings outta the horses. No gewgaws on us at all. See how thorough the lawmen search. Then we find the places they're not looking and start smuggling it out of town, a few bits at a time. Stash the goods someplace, some hidy-hole. Then pack up and leave town clean as a whistle; no one chasing us.' He was grinning as he finished speaking, his gold tooth shining.

Tomcat was the first to react. 'I like that a heap better than shooting lawmen. I vote we give it a whirl.' He raised his beer glass by way of salute.

Black Elliot's grin grew wider as Irish nodded agreement. He was going to pull this one off, and he was going to make a fat profit. When the others saw the cash in their pockets, they'd do anything he asked in future. He looked expectantly at Curly Joe.

Curly nodded slowly, reluctant to give in to Elliot's ideas again. Black Elliot didn't miss the sullen look in Curly Joe's eyes but blandly concealed his own thoughts. Curly would get his fair pay-off, Elliot wasn't about to risk crossing him unnecessarily, but he wouldn't be along on Elliot's next job. Elliot raised his beer glass too.

'Here's to getting the job done.'

'Amen,' replied Irish.

Somewhat revived by food, a wash and clean clothes, Hugh left the sheriff's office to continue searching the town. Edison was sitting on the bench under the office window, stroking Homer as the half-grown cat dozed beside him.

'Where are we searching today?' Edison asked, scratching his stubble.

'The new residential area to the north of town,' Hugh told him.

'Ain't that where you and Minnie are setting up house?' Edison asked.

'Yes, on Walnut Street.' Hugh answered, grimacing slightly at the name. With his battered hat, well-worn boots and his usual air of mild anxiety, he didn't much look like a prominent and wealthy citizen of the town.

Govan had weathered the Panic of 1873 without too much harm, and the town had boomed in the last year or so. It had been decided that a prosperous town needed to offer suitable homes for the wealthier folk it intended to attract and produce, so two streets of fine houses had been laid out on a rise to the north of the town. Walnut Street and Willow Street offered substantial houses with bay windows, stained glass around the entrance, and a room or two for live-in servants. After a ten-minute walk, Hugh breasted the rise and stopped at the end of Walnut

Street, ostensibly to admire the rows of houses, but also to get his breath back. He coughed, still slightly troubled by the smoke he'd breathed in during the fire. Edison let out a low whistle of appreciation.

'Now get an eyeful of those!' he exclaimed. 'I bet Minnie never figgered she'd be setting up home anyplace as fancy as that.'

'Well, she is,' Hugh said proudly. He pointed down the street. 'It's that one, with the green fence out front.' Thoughts of the wedding reminded him what they had come to this area for. 'We'd better get on and start searching.'

They worked methodically up one side of the street, searching the grounds of the new houses for any sign of the stolen jewellery. About a third of the houses were occupied; some were still being finished. The gardens were still raw; some had newly planted saplings and shrubs that looked rather forlorn in the rough, uncultivated ground that surrounded them. Hugh realized with dismay that the loose soil around new plantings would have been a tempting possibility for someone wanting to bury something in a hurry, without leaving obvious traces. He borrowed a couple of shovels, and with Edison's help, spent two hot hours digging around the roots of new plants. The owner of one house refused to give permission for his new garden to be dug up. Hugh was hot, tired and thirsty. He almost lost his temper, and threatened to arrest the householder for obstructing the law. After a fierce exchange of threats, Hugh got his way and searched the garden. Afterwards, Hugh declared that he needed a rest, and proposed a visit to his own house.

'Minnie will probably be there,' he told Edison. 'She's been taking over the bed linen and china, and that sort of thing.'

The wide front door was standing open to let in the prairie breeze. Hugh climbed the steps to the porch and entered, calling to announce his presence.

'Minnie? Are you there?' He stopped half-way along the hall to glance into the parlour.

'Oh, Hugh!' Minnie emerged from the green baize door that separated the front of the house from the kitchen, pantry and scullery at the back. She was wearing one of her older calico dresses, with the sleeves pushed up and a large apron swathing her trim figure. 'Are you all right?' she asked anxiously as she came to meet him. 'I heard you were ambushed and caught in a fire this morning.'

Hugh ignored the damp spots on the apron and hugged her tightly. She felt good in his arms, warm and reassuring.

'I feel better for seeing you,' he said, his mouth close to her ear. Hugh pressed his face against her tightly-pinned coil of dark-blond hair, and revelled in the wholesome smell of soap and the scent of a woman's skin. He forgot Edison's presence until Minnie noticed the other man and suddenly tensed. Hugh reluctantly released her. 'We've been searching this street, but we've come here for a drink.'

'There's only water, I'm afraid,' Minnie said to Edison. 'But it's pumped fresh from the well, so it's good and cold.'

She led the men into the kitchen, where she had been cleaning windows left dirty after the building work, and filled glasses from the pump at the sink.

'Will you come into the parlour?' Minnie asked her guest as she handed him his glass.

Edison took the heavy glass carefully, and shook his head.

'I reckon I won't, Miss Minnie, I'll be happier here. You-all go and jaw some in private.'

Hugh had downed his glass of water in one go. He followed Minnie along to the parlour, where he sank on to the sofa with a sigh of relief. She sat alongside him and took his hand. Hugh winced slightly; his hands were sore from the fire and the digging.

'Sorry.' Minnie held his broad-palmed hand in her smaller one and examined the red, blistered skin. 'You should soak those in cold water and let me bind them up before you leave,' she said.

'It shows how little manual work I do,' Hugh commented.

'You're a gentleman, not a labourer,' Minnie said simply.

'You're a lady, with or without a title,' Hugh answered.

He leaned over to kiss her. Minnie responded warmly, her mouth soft and yielding beneath his. He kissed her again, forgetting his sore hands as he pulled her close. Cares were forgotten for a few minutes as Hugh lost himself in the sensations of kissing and holding. The comfort of another human, loving presence, was what he needed. When they released one another, Hugh kept hold of her hand.

He glanced at the blisters on his free hand.

'I damn nearly got killed this morning,' he said quietly. 'Archer nearly killed me the other night.' He reached up and touched the scar on the side of his head, mostly hidden by hair. The bullet that had left its mark there had been within an inch of killing or crippling him. 'Darrow's driving us all to madness, trying to run the town, run a blockade and search for the bloody jewels, all at the same time. Why should I work for him any more? I want to live here with you, and have a family and eat well and get fat, and have a long life. I don't want to get shot; I've got better things to do with my life.' He ran out of words and simply stared at Minnie.

Minnie reached up and gently touched his scar too.

'You got that doing your duty.'

'My duty,' Hugh repeated. 'Richard and I used to hear so much about that. My ancestors went on the Crusades, they've fought battles in half the countries of Europe, as well as China, India and America. Go back far enough and you'll find barons and earls in my family tree, and even a distant great-grand-what-ever-aunt who became a duchess. Richard and I were always being made to look at portraits and being told how whoever-it-was had earned their title or land.' Hugh fell silent suddenly, lost in thought. Minnie waited patiently and watched, as he looked around the room at the new furnishings, the thick curtains, the wallpaper and the pictures.

'They earned it,' Hugh said again. 'They earned their wealth by doing their duty, and because of that,

I eventually inherited a comfortable income and a bit of land in Norfolk. Have I earned that?'

'You've been deputy in Govan for five years now. You've worked hard and risked your life to make this a good place to live,' Minnie answered. 'That scar is proof of that. The way this town has boomed is proof too. Businesses and settlers are moving here because Govan has good law. Sheriff Darrow didn't do it all on his own. He'd miss you if you quit altogether,' she added.

'You wouldn't get him to admit it under torture,' Hugh said promptly.

Minnie laughed and got a wry smile in return.

'Darrow gave me his word that marrying you was the best thing I could do,' Hugh said. 'And he was right. I don't know what I did to deserve you, but I won't let you down.' His eyes shone brighter as he looked at her. 'I want you to be proud of me, Minnie, and I know you'll be prouder of a man that earns his place and respect, than one who runs away from things.'

'Remember the first time we met?' Minnie asked. 'You climbed on to the roof of our stable to rescue my little brother. I could see you were scared, but you did it anyway. I admired you for that, and now I love you, and I'm proud of you.'

Hugh was lost for an answer, but he felt a sudden rush of confidence and joy. He expressed himself by taking hold of Minnie and kissing her passionately. Minnie was slightly breathless when Hugh finally took his lips from hers. She gasped as he gently kissed her cheek, and started trailing kisses down the sensitive skin of her neck. Hugh could feel her trembling as he kissed lower, her breath coming faster. Minnie shivered and made a soft sound of pleasure as he kissed the hollow as the base of her throat.

Soft chimes from the French clock on the mantelpiece interrupted them. Hugh reluctantly lifted his head from Minnie's neck and glanced at the clock.

'Oh, my Lord!' he exclaimed. 'I've got to go and get ready for that inquest on bloody Archer.'

Minnie swallowed and made a visible effort to pull herself together. Her face was prettily flushed and her blue eyes were shining.

'I guess you'd better hurry,' she said.

Hugh helped her to stand up.

'Will you tell Edison where I've gone? He might as well search around here, and the empty houses at the end of the street.'

Minnie nodded; she accompanied Hugh to the front door and kissed him, more chastely, on the porch. She leaned close and whispered to him:

'You know what I'm looking forward to most about our wedding day?'

Hugh looked at her expectantly, and Minnie smiled.

'Our wedding night.' She stepped back inside and closed the wide door, still smiling.

Hugh bounced down the steps, walking taller than when he had arrived, and whistled merrily as he went.

# CHAPTER TEN

Tomcat Billy volunteered to be the first to try out Black Elliot's new plan. Being forced to stay in the town was starting to make him edgy, and he needed to reassure himself that he could move on if he wanted to. His share of the jewellery was safe with Irish for the afternoon. His friend intended to do nothing more exciting than sit in the drugstore and read a newspaper. As he let his mare, Sarah, pick her way across the railroad tracks, Tomcat studied the blockade the sheriff had set up just beyond the Red Arrow Haulage Company. A double pole arrangement had been set up across the dry trail. A shorter section could be opened to let a rider or a person on foot through; the main width had to be opened to let a wagon through. Tomcat rode slowly towards the barrier and halted as the sheriff moved to meet him. Another man, a lean fellow with intense eyes and a villainous moustache, stayed by the barricade with a shotgun resting in his arms, and watched.

'Afternoon, Sheriff,' Tomcat said pleasantly. 'I'm taking Sarah here out to stretch her legs some, and find me a place for a swim.' As he spoke, he studied the face of the man who was hunting him. Sheriff Darrow was beginning to need a shave and there were lines of weariness in his face, but Tomcat looked at the other man's eyes. He saw a strength of will there that he'd never seen in Black Elliot.

'Will you dismount, please?' the sheriff drawled.

Tomcat slid his feet from the stirrups and dismounted gracefully. 'I done read the notice at the livery barn,' he said. 'I know youn's be fixin' to search me.'

'And the horse,' the sheriff said. He gestured to the other man. 'Josh?'

Tomcat surrendered his reins to the deputy. At the sheriff's request, he took off his brown corduroy jacket and his worn gunbelt, with the short-bladed knife and Civilian model Peacemaker. He stood quietly and watched as the sheriff searched both thoroughly, feeling the hem and lapels of the jacket as well as the pockets. The gunbelt was inspected for concealed compartments; the revolver and knife were removed and holster and sheath checked, though there would barely be room for an earring in either. The movements were quick and practised; the sheriff had developed a routine for searching that was thorough without wasting time.

Tomcat also paid some attention to the man searching his mare. First his canteen was shaken, then emptied into an enamel jug. The deputy could see at a glance that there was nothing besides water in the canteen. He poured it back in, fastened the lid, and tied it back to the saddle. The small roll behind the saddle was taken down and carefully undone. It was just a towel and Tomcat's washkit, along with a couple of bread rolls and a piece of cooked sausage wrapped in paper. The deputy, Josh, glanced over the food and the contents of the washkit before putting them back as he'd found them. Tomcat wondered if he could hide a brooch or even a necklace in some sort of food. He quickly squashed the thought, concentrating on cheerful thoughts about riding and swimming.

'Hold out your arms, please,' the sheriff asked.

Tomcat again did as he was asked. 'I hear tell it's some jewellery you're looking for,' he remarked.

'There's a reward for it,' the sheriff answered, as he felt his way along Tomcat's arms and down his body. 'One thousand dollars.'

Tomcat whistled. 'If the reward's that high, them must be some mighty purty stones.'

'They may be worth more to the Keatings than on the open market,' the sheriff said.

Darrow felt around the waistband of Tomcat's trousers, then downwards to the knee-high moccasins.

'Careful there, Sheriff,' Tomcat quipped. 'There's some places I normally reserve for the gentle touch of a woman.'

Humour gleamed briefly in the sheriff's dark eyes.

'That's the first time I ever had a man ask me to go gently with him.'

Tomcat grinned and relaxed as the sheriff stood up and moved away.

'Thank you for your co-operation,' the sheriff said, handing back Tomcat's gunbelt and jacket.

Tomcat buckled the gunbelt on first. 'My momma always told me to be polite to a man wearing a fancy badge,' he said, pulling on his jacket again in spite of the hot weather.

'I'd guess your momma didn't raise any fools,' the sheriff said, moving to open the barricade. Tomcat mounted lightly and took his reins from the deputy.

'My momma done raised eleven smart kids,' he answered proudly. He nudged his horse into a walk and was through the barrier before turning in the saddle to add: 'But I was born twelfth!'

Hugh was packing his battered iron-bound trunk when Darrow returned to their rooms above the sheriff's office that evening. When he heard Darrow's footsteps on the wooden stairs, Hugh left his bedroom, a folded shirt still in his hands. Darrow shrugged his black jacket off and laid it over the back of the easy chair nearest the top of the stairs. Without paying any attention to Hugh, he unbuckled his gunbelt and laid that over the jacket. Moving slowly, Darrow made his way to the rocking-chair opposite and sat down. The high chairback hid Darrow's face from Hugh's sight. Hugh quietly walked into the kitchen end of the room, leaving the folded shirt on the dining table, and put the coffee pot on the stove.

The coffee was starting to bubble and smell good, when there was a thunder of paws on the stairs. Homer came running up, his eyes bright and his tail aloft. The cat trotted over to the rocking-chair and jumped carefully into Darrow's lap. He turned around and settled down, purring vigorously. When the coffee was done, Hugh put a frypan on the stove to start warming, and took two mugs of coffee across the room. He handed one to Darrow and sat in the easy chair with the other.

'Thank you.' It was the first thing Darrow had said since his return.

Only here, with no one but Hugh to see, could Darrow allow himself to relax. Lines of mental and physical weariness were etched into his face. He sipped at his coffee, and stroked Homer with his free hand.

'Edison and I searched the length of Walnut Street today,' Hugh said. 'We didn't find anything more than a couple of nickels that someone had dropped.' He paused for a moment. 'We've searched just about this whole town now.'

'I swear that jewellery is still here,' Darrow said, life returning to his tired face. 'I can't see how anyone could have got it out of town.'

'Someone told Richard about the Pinkertons, and he says he might hire them to find it.'

Darrow scowled. 'This is *my* town; I don't want any detective company doing my job here.'

'But if the jewellery has been smuggled out, you can't go chasing after it,' Hugh pointed out. 'You've only got jurisdiction within this county, and now Govan's so big, you can't leave it to run itself while you chase jewellery thieves.'

Darrow didn't answer, but his expression showed that he knew Hugh was right.

'I think you're right about the thieves still being here,' Hugh went on. He leaned back in his chair and discovered the sheriff's gunbelt draped uncomfortably behind him. Sitting up again, he carried on talking. 'Whoever set that trap this morning baited it with the jet earrings, remember? They're still in town and they're getting scared. They can't relax while we're out looking for them, as well anyone who wants the reward.'

Darrow frowned at the mention of the reward. Hugh sensibly stopped talking and let him think.

'I spoke to someone this afternoon about the reward,' Darrow recalled. 'Someone I've surely seen around town recently.' The sheriff's eyes suddenly brightened. 'It was that hill-billy; it was the way he spoke about "them purty stones".' Darrow turned his own drawl into an imitation of Tomcat's thicker accent. 'I remember seeing him before, on Monday. Him and three others came to the depot but only one of them got the train; it was the first one after the robbery. The one that got on was a big, fair-haired man with a touch of an Irish accent. He claimed to be a labourer but he surely hadn't done any rough work for some time. The hill-billy I saw this afternoon was with him and two others at the depot then. One of them was a half-caste, carrying a carpet bag.'

'There's no law against carpet bags,' Hugh remarked. 'What does the hill-billy look like?'

'A couple of inches shorter than you; slim, green eyes, brown hair, clean-shaved.' Darrow said. 'Wore brown, apart from a yellow neckerchief, and wears knee-high moccasins. Brown gunbelt with a short-barrelled Colt and a knife. Surely not more than twenty-two. Rides a brown mare with lots of white on the legs and looks like he spends a lot of time outdoors.'

'I think I've seen him somewhere,' Hugh mused. 'Him and that big, fair-haired fellow.' A few moments' effort failed to produce the memory. Hugh sipped his coffee and looked at Darrow, who was rubbing Homer's ear. 'Bacon with fried apples and onions all right for supper?' He knew perfectly well that it was one of Darrow's favourite dishes.

Darrow smiled; a rare heartfelt smile that warmed his eyes and lifted some of the strain from his face.

'Well now, that would be fine, thank you.'

Hugh smiled back and went to start supper, feeling a little brighter himself.

The next morning, it was Hugh's turn to stay in the office. The windows and the door were propped open as usual. Hugh didn't mind the noise that came in with the breeze, he preferred company to solitude and frequently looked up from his work to listen to snatches of conversation that came through the window. Mid-morning, Hugh's attention was caught by a voice that seemed to be speaking right outside the window nearest the desk.

'Morning, my ginger friend. See what Tomcat done saved you from his breakfast.' Something about the voice caught his attention. Hugh chewed absently on the end of his pen as he listened and tried to make the connection.

'You'd look mighty fine with some purty jewels round your neck, Tiger,' the voice drawled. Hugh realized with a start that the man talking outside had the thick hill-billy accent that Darrow had briefly imitated the night before. He stood up slowly, careful not to let the chair scrape on the wooden floor, and moved quietly to where he could see through the window better. There was a bench on the sidewalk beneath the window. Hugh could see the profile of a man looking down at something on the bench beside him. The brown cloth cap and general appearance matched the description Darrow had given of the hill-billy.

Hugh's mind worked in a series of quick leaps. He knew at once that he had seen this man before, but he couldn't immediately remember when. He tended to forget what had happened when he was drunk and the only time recently he'd got well and truly drunk was on his stag night. Hugh's eyes widened as the memory returned. This man and the big, fair-haired one had been in the Empty Lode that night; he had included them in the first round of drinks. A second memory popped up; some kind of speech about Minnie being worth more than rubies, and jewels being brought for her dowry.

Now Hugh began thinking fast. He could hear the rattle of a badly-laden wagon approaching. As it passed the window, Hugh used the cover of the noise it made to move away from the window, picking up a deck of cards from a shelf at the back of the room as he went. Hugh knew that Darrow had searched this man yesterday, but that had been at the blockade. Anyone leaving town would expect to be searched. Right now, the sheriff was, as usual, at the blockade by the rail depot, with Richard. Pacey was searching the north of town, with Edison. Hugh checked the Webley in its holster, and stepped out on to the sidewalk.

Now Hugh could see the other man properly. He was sitting on the bench, feeding scraps of bacon rind to Homer as the cat lazed in the sunshine. Hugh couldn't see Tomcat's face, but he could see the yellow neckerchief and the long moccasins that Darrow had described.

'I see you like our cat,' Hugh said in a friendly tone.

Tomcat turned to look at him, his green eyes shaded by the peak of his cap.

'I were just giving him some bacon,' he said defensively. 'I wouldn't do no harm to any cat, and that's a fact.'

Hugh smiled. 'His name's Homer. I found him lost in the snow around Christmas and brought him home. He'd almost frozen to death.'

'That was a mighty Christian thing to do,' Tomcat said. He glanced at the cat and rubbed its ear. Hugh leaned casually against the wall of the office, his hands in his pockets.

'I've seen you before,' he said conversationally. 'Weren't you in the Empty Lode when I was having my bachelor party?'

'I was.' Tomcat smiled now. 'And you were surely generous. I never saw no one put two fifty-dollar bills on a bar 'fore now.'

'They vanished fast enough,' Hugh replied. 'I'm good at making money vanish,' he added. He stood up straight and took his hands from his pockets, showing a dime in his right hand. 'See that?' Tomcat nodded, a little wary but curious.

'I had to take bills, because I'd have needed to take saddlebags full of coins if I wanted to pay for all the drinks in silver.' As Hugh started his patter, he changed the coin from hand to hand. 'And I can't afford to buy any saddlebags.' He deftly palmed the dime as Tomcat laughed, then opened both hands to show them empty.

Tomcat's face lit up. 'That's swell!'

'I am a talented practitioner of predestigitation,' Hugh announced, enjoying the success of the simple trick. 'Would you like to know where the dime went?'

'Sure.'

Hugh gestured for the other man to stand up. 'The object summoned or sent finds its own resting place,' he said gravely. 'I have to listen carefully in order to locate the missing object.' He moved closer to Tomcat, his head on one side. 'Do you know where it might be?' While Tomcat was thinking about that, Hugh 'produced' the coin from Tomcat's right ear.

This time Tomcat applauded. Hugh was aware that one or two others had stopped, but he concentrated solely on the man in front of him.

'There must be something magical about you,' Hugh said. 'What's your name?'

'Tomcat Billy,' Tomcat answered unguardedly.

'Ah. Cats are magical creatures. The Ancient Egyptians worshipped them as gods, you know,' Hugh said, swapping the coin for the deck of cards he'd picked up. He handed the pack to Tomcat and asked him to shuffle them.

For the next couple of minutes, Hugh showed off some of his best card tricks and sleight of hand skills. A dozen or so people gathered to watch, some of whom had more important things to do, but they got drawn in by Hugh's skill and patter. As always, Hugh responded to an audience, cracking jokes and keeping everyone laughing. All the time, he used Tomcat as the centre of his tricks. The temptation to continue was strong, but Hugh had had a good reason for showing off. The thunder of two cowhands galloping up Main Street gave him the chance to finish the show.

'I want everyone to close their eyes,' he called. 'And everyone must repeat their name over and again, but quietly.' Hugh took a quick glance at the crowd, and saw they were doing as he asked. Another look showed him that Tomcat was doing the same. The murmuring of the voices and the sound of the hoofs were enough to muffle the quiet but distinctive sound of a gun being drawn. Hugh stepped back, so he was just out of arm's reach from Tomcat, and pointed his Webley straight at the unsuspecting man.

'Stop!' he called, thumbing back the trigger as he spoke. 'Tomcat Billy, I'm arresting you for the possession of stolen goods.'

Tomcat opened his green eyes very wide. He took one glance at the powerful handgun aimed at his chest, and stayed still.

'What stolen goods?' he asked, speaking above the shocked exclamations of the onlookers.

Hugh dipped his left hand into his jacket pocket

and produced a bracelet that glittered in the sunshine. 'I lifted this from your pocket just now when I was doing a trick. There's plenty more in there.' The excited voices of the crowd, and the exclamations at the jewellery, went to Hugh's head. He grinned, and held the bracelet up so the crowd could have a better view of it. 'Kennick!' He called to a teamster he had recognized in the crowd. 'Come up behind him and remove his gunbelt.'

In spite of the temptation to turn to the people offering congratulations, Hugh kept his eyes firmly on his prisoner as Kennick stepped up on to the sidewalk behind Tomcat, and reached around him to unfasten his gunbelt. Hugh told someone else to fetch the sheriff, then marched his prisoner into the office at gunpoint. Kennick followed, carrying the gunbelt as an excuse to see what happened next.

Inside the office, Hugh told Kennick to put the gunbelt on the desk, then to take off Tomcat's jacket. Tomcat made no resistance, fully aware of the handgun aimed steadily at him. Kennick whistled as he slipped the worn jacket from Tomcat's narrow shoulders, and felt its weight.

'He's carrying something around in this,' the teamster remarked, laying the jacket over the desk.

'Thank you.' Hugh looked at his prisoner: Tomcat hadn't moved an inch from where he'd been told to stand. He was keeping his face very still but his rapid breathing betrayed his anxiety.

'Want for me to search this?' Kennick asked, indicating the jacket.

Hugh shook his head. 'I'll wait for Darrow.'

He didn't need to wait for long, as running foot-steps outside announced the arrival of the sheriff. Darrow entered, breathing a little heavily after his run, and took in the situation at a glance.

'I haven't searched my prisoner yet,' Hugh said smugly to Darrow. 'I thought I'd wait and let you give a hand. He's called Tomcat Billy.'

Darrow ignored him. 'Put your hands together behind your back,' he ordered Tomcat.

With Darrow in the room, and the prisoner hand-cuffed, Hugh felt it was safe to holster his gun. He picked up the jacket and began searching the pockets. Kennick gave a soft exclamation as Hugh produced the jewellery: bracelets and rings tangled together, an amethyst necklace in a silk pouch. Hugh piled the jewellery carefully on the wooden desk. Under Darrow's watchful eye, he searched Tomcat thoroughly, producing a box containing four pairs of earrings from one trouser pocket. When he had finished, Darrow told him to lock Tomcat's gunbelt and the recovered jewellery in the safe.

'You can go now,' he told Kennick.

The teamster looked at the sheriff's dark expression and took the hint.

When the door had closed behind Kennick, Darrow moved to face the handcuffed prisoner. Hugh stood slightly behind him and to one side, leaning against the desk as he watched. Darrow took a step closer to Tomcat, his face cold and set as he glared at the smaller man.

'Tell us where your friends are, Tomcat,' Darrow demanded.

Tomcat Billy looked down at the dusty wooden floor, his mouth firmly shut.

'You ride with that big Irishman, a half-caste and another man. I saw you-all together the day of the robbery,' Darrow went on, his slow drawl somehow emphasizing the threat in his eyes. His muscles were tight as his temper began to rise and burn.

Tomcat glanced at the sheriff and spoke briefly. 'I don't know nuthin'.'

Darrow lashed out with a back-handed slap that rocked Tomcat back a step. Hugh watched with wide eyes as Darrow advanced on his prisoner.

'They're not worth protecting,' Darrow snapped. 'I want their names.'

Tomcat shook his head and tensed, preparing himself for another blow.

Darrow reached out fast with his left hand, grabbing the front of Tomcat's shirt and pulling him close. With the other hand, he drew his Colt and rammed the end of the barrel into Tomcat's stomach.

Hugh straightened up, but held back his intended protest. Tomcat's eyes were wide with fear as he stared into the sheriff's stony face.

'You ever seen a man get belly-shot?' Darrow asked, his voice low. 'I saw it during the War. A man can take hours, even a day or more, to bleed to death from being gut-shot. It hurts like hell.' He clicked back the hammer of the Colt. 'Tell me your friends' names, and where I can find them.' Tomcat swallowed and opened his mouth. He made an effort to control his panicky gasps for breath.

'It was Black Elliot's idea,' he blurted out. 'Him and Curly Joe are over at the White Buffalo.'

Darrow gave the small man a quick shake. 'What about your Irish friend?'

Tomcat hesitated; Darrow slid the muzzle of the gun down until it rested against his prisoner's groin.

'Tell me, Tomcat. Or you won't be siring any more bastard kittens.'

Tomcat blinked and licked his dry lips.

'He's at Mrs Parkin's boarding house,' he whispered.

Darrow moved his gun so it was pointing at the floor, and carefully lowered the trigger. Behind him, Hugh let out a sigh of relief. Darrow holstered his revolver, then released his hold on Tomcat's shirt and ordered him to turn around.

Tomcat made no attempt to escape as he was put in the cell and his handcuffs removed. Hugh made sure the cell door was locked securely and followed Darrow back to the outer office without another glance at the prisoner. Darrow spared a brief glance for his deputy, who picked up a shotgun and began loading it.

Hugh was fretting as usual. 'Should we send someone to let the others know what's going on? There's no point in Richard and Louisa searching the carnival if Tomcat's friends are carrying the jewellery around with them. I'd rather we outnumbered the men we're going to arrest.'

'We'll pick up Josh on our way past his place,' Darrow said. 'Now move.'

# CHAPTER ELEVEN

Tomcat Billy took a deep breath, and tried to calm his racing heartbeat. His imagination could still feel the pressure of the revolver's muzzle against his belly. He'd spilt out the real names in his first rush of fear, but had managed to hold himself together sufficiently to lie about where his comrades were. The misdirection would buy him a little time, and he had to make the most of it.

As soon as he heard the outer door of the office closing behind the lawmen, Tomcat moved to the bunk. He unknotted the yellow neckerchief, and carefully unrolled it on the woollen bed-blanket. The faded fabric revealed short pieces of metal: Tomcat's lockpicks. Each pick was made in two pieces that screwed together, as ordinary lockpicks would be too long to fit easily around the curve of his neck. These were hardly bigger than matchsticks and were well concealed in the tight roll of his neckerchief.

Tomcat's slim, agile fingers neatly assembled the picks. A couple of paces brought him to the front of the steel-barred cell. He slipped his arms between the bars and started work on the lock. All the time he was manoeuvring the picks in the lock, he was also listening for anyone returning to the office. Tomcat bit on his lower lip as he prised with the picks, trying not to think about how much time was passing. It seemed far longer than a couple of minutes before he felt the lock give way, and heard it click open.

It took less than a minute to take the lockpicks apart again, and to roll them up in the yellow neckerchief. Tomcat settled it around his neck, smiling to himself as he knotted the age-softened fabric. The cell door moved quietly on its hinges as he pushed it open and stepped through. He shivered briefly, a reaction to the hated feeling of being locked up. Tomcat valued his painstakingly learned lock-picking skills more for their use in getting him out of places, than for getting him in. Tomcat resisted the temptation to try and retrieve his gunbelt, and maybe some jewellery, and went straight to the rear door. It opened when he tried it, so Tomcat stepped casually from the lawmen's building, and closed the door after himself as anyone would.

A minute later, Tomcat was out back of Pinder's Hotel. He sprinted across the yard and bounded up on to the stable roof with an ease that seemed to deny the existence of gravity. A few moments later he was sliding in through Black Elliot's window.

'What in hell!' Elliot cut off his loud exclamation at Tomcat's dramatic arrival. He almost dropped the book he had been reading and stood up.

'The sheriff's looking for you-all.' Tomcat spoke fast, forestalling the explosion of anger from Elliot that would cost time. 'That fancy-speaking English deputy tricked me and arrested me. They left me locked in a cell while they went looking for the rest of youns,' he added.

Elliot didn't bother asking how Tomcat had got out of the cell.

'You went and told them our names, you little skunk?'

Tomcat glared back at him. 'That sheriff had his gun pressed 'gainst my belly and he was mad enough to spit nails. I bought us some time, anyhow; I done sent him looking in the wrong places.'

'I'm glad to know you got some sense between your ears,' Elliot snapped. 'You know whereabouts Irish is?'

Tomcat nodded, biting back what he wanted to say. He watched Elliot thinking hard. The coloured man brought his harmonica from his pocket and turned it over a few times as he came to a decision.

'There's no point hiding no more,' Elliot went on. 'We'll get the horses and run two ways. That sheriff is in charge and he can't be in two places together. You and Irish make a run through the carnival; me and Curly'll head out east and go cross-country that ways.'

'Where we going to meet?' Tomcat asked, looking the other man straight in the eyes. 'They done took my share and my gunbelt. I left them in the jail to get here quick to you and I'm near 'bout broke.'

'Make for Colorado; Greeley.' Elliot fished a few dollars from his pocket and handed them over.

Tomcat took the money. 'I'll find it.' The thought that he expected to find Black Elliot there, too, was clear enough.

Without wasting any more time, Tomcat Billy slipped out the way he had entered. He retraced his route at a jog, slowing only to stalk along the alley between the sheriff's office and the grocery store. Tomcat scanned the street warily from the end of the alley, before nipping out. As he'd hoped, Irish was inside the drugstore, drinking a soda and slowly reading a newspaper.

'Sure and I'm getting better at reading,' Irish remarked, folding the paper untidily. The smile faded as he looked longer at his friend and saw Tomcat's expression.

'Drink up quick,' Tomcat said quietly. 'We're heading for the hills.'

Irish picked up his glass. 'Where's your iron?' he asked, before taking a long swig.

'Locked in the law's office,' Tomcat answered briefly. 'Like I was.' He touched the yellow neckerchief around his neck.

Irish knew about the lockpicks concealed there, and got the message. He finished up his drink and followed Tomcat from the drugstore.

Outside, in the noise and bustle of the town, Tomcat could explain more about his visit to Black Elliot and the plans made. In less than a minute, they had separated. Tomcat was on his way to their boarding house, where he planned to retrieve their possessions via the first floor window. To Tomcat, this seemed safer than the risk of meeting lawmen in the hallway or on the other side of a door he couldn't see through. Irish was heading to Francis's Livery Stables to saddle the horses.

\*

Sheriff Darrow and Hugh went first to Josh Turnage's funeral parlour on the other side of the main cross-roads from the law office. They found Josh in his stables, grooming one of the black horses he adored. Josh grinned at Hugh's account of how he had arrested Tomcat, then went to change out of his stable clothes, and to pick up his shotgun. He took less than five minutes, but by then, Tomcat was already talking to Black Elliot in Pinder's Hotel.

Mrs Parkin's boarding house was only a minute's walk from the funeral parlour. Mrs Parkin was getting changed into a clean dress after the morning's housework, and kept the lawmen waiting another few minutes. When they did get to speak to her, they discovered Tomcat's lie.

'I'll get the truth from that damned alley-cat if I have to hang him up by his own guts,' Darrow swore, as he left the boarding house.

'Why don't we just check the other boarding houses and hotels?' Hugh asked, hurrying to keep up with the sheriff. 'We know who we're looking for now.'

'If he didn't lie about that too,' Darrow answered, striding along the dusty street. 'Besides, there's five hotels, four saloons and seven boarding houses in Govan now. I'm sure as hell not going to visit all of them if I can shake the information from Tomcat first.'

'I can offer to fix him up a nice funeral if he don't co-operate,' Josh remarked.

Darrow glanced at the lean undertaker; there was

a remarkably sinister gleam in Josh's eye.

'That may help yet,' the sheriff said.

When they reached the office, Darrow led the way into the rear of the building where the cells were. He stopped dead on seeing the empty cell, then advanced to the cell and pushed the door. It swung open. Darrow turned on Hugh, who was right behind him.

'Can't you even lock a damn door?' Darrow yelled.

'Of course I can.' Hugh defended himself automatically. 'I definitely gave it a push to test it after I turned the key. I always do; it's a habit.'

'Where are the keys?' Josh asked. 'Maybe one of his friends saw him get arrested, or heard about it, and came to get him out.'

Darrow pushed past Hugh and checked on the keys. They were still locked in the desk drawer.

'No one's tried jimmying the drawer, or had a go at the safe,' Hugh said. He picked the keys from the drawer and deftly unlocked the safe. He let out an audible sigh at seeing the jewellery still inside. 'His gunbelt's still here too.'

'Could someone have picked the lock of the cell?' Josh suggested.

'Well he's gone now, however he got out,' Hugh said. 'What are we going to do?'

'Go after him and his friends. They can't hide here any more; they'll have to run, and we'll be after them,' Darrow said grimly.

Black Elliot and Curly Joe were already at Norman's livery barn. They saddled their horses swiftly, unwilling to waste time even though they were sure that the sheriff was on a wild-goose chase around the hotels and boarding houses. Elliot paid up the amount they owed; he didn't want anyone raising a fuss until the last moment. Yet another fast change of plan was working on his nerves, and he hurried himself and Curly Joe out of the stables. Curly brought his horse alongside, niggling at the chestnut with his heels so it threw up its head and danced around.

'If we're quitting this town, then let's quit, and fast,' he insisted.

Black Elliot threw him a scornful look. 'Don't be a jug-head, Curly. No one takes notice of a man going slow. We start galloping and everyone looks to see. The lawmen don't know us by sight. We keep on these busy streets and we're just part of the crowd.' He spoke firmly, trying to hide his nerves. Elliot had kept his mind on keeping low and not attracting attention all along; he was incapable of changing now. He steered his horse around a laden wagon and turned east on to Cross Street.

Francis's Livery Barn was at the south end of Lincoln Street, not far from the railroad. Tomcat arrived at a jog, with saddlebags slung over both shoulders. Getting into their boarding house room via the window had been no problem for him. He'd packed their gear swiftly and departed within five minutes, unnoticed by anyone else in the building. Irish had both horses saddled and waiting at the double doors.

'Sure an' I've paid up for the two of us,' he said, taking his saddlebags from Tomcat.

'Thanks.' Tomcat slung his bags behind his saddle and neatly fastened them down. His mare stretched out her neck and shook herself. 'I reckon we should stay off the main street,' he said, lifting his bedroll into place. 'We're both too easy for the law to pick out in a crowd. I say we cut across the end of Main Street, just out of sight of the blockade on the south trail, then cut up by the river.'

'Folks might wonder why we're going that way and not staying on the road,' Irish pointed out, keeping his deep voice low. He finished settling his own bedroll and led his horse outside.

'The sheriff'll be searchin' every hotel, boarding house and saloon in town,' Tomcat answered, following. 'Time anyone's done tracked him down, we'll be clean away and out this damned town.' He vaulted into the saddle and looked across at his friend. Touching the tender spot where Darrow had slapped his face, Tomcat added: 'I can think of just one good reason to come back here someday.'

'It's time to leave now,' Irish answered. He nudged his horse, Frosty, into a walk and led the way.

Their caution was unnecessary; Sheriff Darrow had sent for Deputy Pacey, and told him to get to Norman's livery barn, where the lawmen's horses were stabled. Josh Turnage hurried to his own stables to saddle one of his black horses. Darrow spotted Norman in the saddle room of his livery stable and called to the black man, as he entered.

'Any out-of-towners taken horses today?'

'Sure,' Norman answered, a little startled by the

urgency in the sheriff's voice. 'Two fellers, been in town 'bout a week, rode out just now on their own mounts.'

'Two? What did they look like?' Darrow lifted down his bridle from its peg but kept his attention on the livery barn owner.

In a couple of minutes, he knew that two of the men he was looking for had just left the livery barn, kitted out for travelling some distance. By then, his horse, and Hugh's, were ready, and Norman was saddling Pacey's chestnut gelding.

Pacey arrived at a run sooner than they had expected. Hugh heard him as he was heaving up Cassandra's girths, and was mildly annoyed to realize that Pacey wasn't even out of breath. The three lawmen were mounted and out on the street in next to no time. Darrow took the lead, weaving between wagons to reach Josh at the crossroads. The undertaker called to them as they approached.

'I saw two men with saddlebags and kit heading down east along Cross Street just as I was heading for my stables.'

Darrow halted his horse alongside Josh's.

'Describe them.' He stood in his stirrups and stared along Cross Street as he listened to Josh's description. It matched the two men he had just missed at the livery barn.

'You reckon they're going to meet Tomcat and the Irish fellow outside town?' Hugh asked, recognizing the descriptions too.

'No!' Pacey's exclamation cut off the sheriff's answer. He too was standing in his stirrups, but was looking the other way. 'I can see that big Irishman riding across the end of Cross Street, down by the river. Yes, there's someone else riding alongside of him.'

'They must be heading for the ford and the carnival,' Darrow said. He made his decision instantly. 'Josh and Pacey, go after Tomcat and Irish. Hugh, stay with me.' He sent his horse into a fast trot without waiting to see his orders obeyed.

Hugh turned his chestnut mare and hustled her after the sheriff eastwards along Cross Street.

'This way's quickest,' Josh told Pacey. He headed back up Main Street, then turned sharp left into the alleyway between the Elysian Bath House and the livery stables. Now they were off Main Street, Josh urged his horse into a gallop. Once they had passed the end of the stables, the ford was almost directly ahead. His horse pounded along willingly, its heavy mane and tail lifting in the wind of its speed. Pacey brought his faster horse alongside, and gave a cry of triumph at seeing the two outlaws splashing across the ford.

The sound of their horses' galloping hoofs carried to the outlaws. Tomcat glanced back over his shoulder as Pacey drew his Colt. The outlaws kicked their horses into a gallop, sending up great splashes of water as the horses plunged in their efforts to speed up. Pacey kept his horse going straight and took a long-range shot. He was half-satisfied to see Tomcat flinch, but it was immediately clear that he hadn't hit him.

'Too many folk on the other side,' Josh warned.

'Wait till we're clear of the carnival.'

Pacey holstered his revolver and concentrated on riding his horse into the turbulent waters of the ford.

At the other end of the carnival, Richard and Louisa were at the doll's head booth.

'I'm sure we're wasting our time here,' Richard complained as he crouched behind the array of wooden dolls-heads to examine the ground under the stall. He poked at the yellowed grass half-heartedly, and glanced around at the underneath of the booth. Above him he heard the thunk of wooden balls hitting the dolls' heads, or more often, the gentler sound of them hitting the backdrop. 'I'm longing for a cup of tea,' he grumbled, coming out backwards and standing up.

Louisa didn't answer; she was on tiptoe, looking down between the rows of booths towards the ford. Richard was about to speak when they both heard a gunshot. The crowds nearest the river began to scatter, clearing the way for two riders who were coming at a full gallop.

'What the hell are they doing!' Richard exclaimed. 'That's damned dangerous!'

'Look!' Louisa grabbed his arm. 'I think that's Josh and Pacey chasing them.'

Richard pushed past her to the front of the booth for a better look. He immediately saw that his wife was right, in which case the two men they were chasing must be fugitives.

'Those bastards must be the jewel thieves!' he exclaimed, glaring at the two outlaws.

Tomcat and Irish had almost reached the booth

where Richard and Louisa were standing. They would pass barely five feet away, but Richard's shotgun was behind the stall. Richard cursed, then spun and grabbed two of the wooden balls from the front of the dolls-head booth. He took a couple of steps and hurled one of the balls after the fleeing outlaws. Richard's aim was good. The ball struck Tomcat on the back of the head with an audible crack.

'Well bowled, sir!' yelled Louisa, as Tomcat slumped in his saddle and slid sideways.

Richard ran after the horses, still clutching the other ball. Behind him were Josh Turnage and Pacey, closing fast on their horses, and Louisa, holding up her skirts to run more easily. Ahead of him, he saw the smaller outlaw fall from his horse, but with his right foot tangled in the wide stirrup. The horse kept galloping, dragging the semi-conscious man over the dusty ground. Irish leaned sideways in his saddle, trying to catch the loose reins of Tomcat's horse. He started to slow his own mount, hoping the other horse would slow too, and eventually managed to catch a trailing rein. It hadn't taken long, but by the time he had both horses at a blowing standstill, Tomcat was lying still and silent.

Josh and Pacey slowed their own horses as they approached, not wishing to spook Tomcat's horse into moving while he was still caught up in the stirrup.

'Hold it there!' Pacey's command to Irish was backed by his fancy Colt.

The big man had tied the rein of Tomcat's horse to his own saddle and was about to dismount. There was nothing mild in his broad face as he turned to the deputies.

'Tomcat's hurt, damn you. I gotta see to him.'

'We'll see to him,' Josh answered, raising his shotgun. 'The sooner we get you cuffed and safe, the sooner we'll be taking care of your friend.'

Irish didn't hesitate; he raised his hands and surrendered at once.

# CHAPTER TWELVE

Sheriff Darrow set his black gelding jogging along Cross Street, with Hugh riding behind him as they wove in and out of the carts, wagons and vans. In spite of his impatience, Darrow kept to a trot not only because of the busy street, but because he was wise enough to let the stabled horses warm up gently before settling into what could be an extended chase. There were fewer people around as the lawmen left the stores and businesses behind, passing between the last few lumber houses on the outskirts. Beyond them was simply open, rolling prairie, marked by the faintest of tracks. Darrow stood in his stirrups, hoping to see Black Elliot and Curly Joe. Josh had seen them start along Cross Street, but they could have turned off somewhere and vanished amongst the maze of buildings either side.

'Sheriff! Sheriff!'

Darrow halted his horse at the shouts and looked around to see Edison running towards them from the edge of town.

'What is it?' he snapped.

Edison reached them and stopped, gasping for breath.

'I done saw . . .' He paused for a coughing fit. 'I saw two men ride out of town this way.' He gestured out at the prairie. 'I follered them some way to see where at they was going. One was a dandy-dressed darkie; the other looked kind of like a Mex.'

'Good work,' Darrow said, glancing at Hugh. 'Where were they aiming for?'

'Looked to me like they'd picked that stand of trees out by Plum Bluff, and was heading straight to that,' Edison answered. He was smiling, his face alight at the knowledge of being useful. Darrow nodded and sent his eager horse on again.

'I'll see you get a share of the reward,' Hugh promised the drunk, as he rode away.

The sheriff pushed his horse on into a lope. Hugh followed suit, losing ground slightly. His sturdy chestnut mare, Cassandra, was not as well-bred as the sheriff's horse, and had a shorter stride. Although the prairie seemed level at first, the ground rose and fell in a rolling series of dips. If Black Elliot and Curly Joe were heading to a marker, as Edison thought, they would travel directly, regardless of the ground. Darrow knew exactly where Plum Bluff was, and could choose his route. He kept them to a ridge of higher ground that ran slightly to the south of the line the outlaws would be taking. Hugh didn't ask questions, but sat quietly, nursing his horse's strength, and scanned the sparsely wooded land ahead of them.

Just a couple of minutes later, they both saw two

horsemen appearing out of a dip, less than a mile ahead. The outlaws were moving at a slow trot as their horses climbed the long slope. As they reached the higher ground, one man glanced back over his shoulder. He looked over his left shoulder, however, and didn't see the two lawmen who were well off to his right. Darrow's expression became more intense; the look of a hunter glowing in his dark eyes. He let the black stride out faster, keeping to the higher, more level ground as much as possible so the horses could keep a more even pace.

The lawmen were within 400 yards of the outlaws before they were spotted. Black Elliot glanced about as he reached a long spur of high ground, and saw the two riders a short distance behind and off to one side. The outlaws changed direction for the first time since leaving town, swinging away from the lawmen at an angle and speeding into a gallop. Darrow leaned in his saddle, letting the black horse turn in a wide circle to follow the outlaws. He gestured to Hugh, some twenty yards behind, telling his deputy not to close up, but to keep the same distance apart.

They galloped on in this way for nearly a mile, the lawmen keeping much the same distance behind the two outlaws. They were circling around to the north of Govan, although the town itself was mostly out of sight, down by the river. Sheriff Darrow knew exactly where he was, and that he had the outlaws where he wanted them. His horse, Gabriel, was galloping steadily, ignoring a jack rabbit that leapt up almost under his hoofs. The horse's coat was damp with sweat, but when the sheriff asked him for more, the black stretched out his neck and found extra speed. Hugh was on the sheriff's left, and already slightly behind. Since leaving town, he had had confidence in Darrow's ability to solve the problem of catching the fleeing outlaws. Now, recognizing the ground ahead of them, Hugh knew what the sheriff had planned. He too urged a further burst of speed from his horse.

They halved the distance between themselves and the outlaws before the move was noticed. The drumming of hoofs on the dry prairie almost drowned out the shrill barks of alarmed prairie dogs not far away. Darrow smiled grimly at the sound as he watched the outlaws ahead. The fleeing men were urging their horses on, trying to regain their lead. Darrow looped his reins loosely around the saddle horn, and drew his Winchester from its boot. The black ran on straight as Darrow rose and braced himself in his stirrups, lifting the rifle to his shoulder. He knew the range was too far for anything but a lucky hit, especially from his galloping horse, but the sheriff wanted to worry the outlaws. He wanted them thinking about the lawmen behind them, not the ground ahead.

Sure enough, the shots had no visible effect other than making Black Elliot glance over his shoulder. A few moments later, Curly's horse suddenly turned in a dramatic somersault. Its hind legs kicked against the sky as it rolled over, throwing its rider clear. As Darrow had hoped, the outlaws hadn't noticed that they were being driven towards the abandoned outskirts of the prairie-dog town. The horse had put one leg in the entrance to an old burrow and come down. Curly Joe hit the ground and rolled over a few times, but was quickly sitting up. His horse was struggling to rise, but its foreleg was broken. It whinnied pitifully as it staggered up on to its three sound legs, and stood with its head hanging and the injured leg raised so only the toe of the hoof touched the ground.

'Elliot! Elliot!' Curly Joe was yelling at the other outlaw. 'Come back here, you yellow son-of-a-bitch!' Curly drew his revolvers. He fired one wild shot after Black Elliot, then turned on the approaching lawmen.

'Throw down your guns and surrender!' Sheriff Darrow ordered. He had slowed his horse to a steady lope and was guiding the black with his legs, keeping both hands free to aim his rifle. Off to his left, Hugh was doing the same.

'Goddam you!' Curly yelled back. 'I'll see you in Hell!' He aimed and fired, but his Colts didn't have the range to worry the sheriff.

Darrow halted his blowing horse, and raised his rifle to his shoulder.

'Drop them or I'll shoot.'

Curly threw down his revolvers and lunged towards his horse, aiming to grab his rifle. Darrow fired once and saw the outlaw stagger slightly. Curly seized the butt of his rifle and tried to haul it from its boot. The sheriff changed his aim slightly and shot Curly's horse. The chestnut buckled and collapsed at once, falling towards the outlaw. Curly jumped out of the way, cursing as his rifle was trapped under the body of the horse. Frustrated, and abandoned by Elliot, Curly Joe lost all sense. He dived towards his revolvers, determined to do whatever damage he could.

'I'll kill you all, you sons-of-bitches!' he screamed, grabbing his guns. 'I'll wring that cursed alleycat's neck, and I'll track down that yellow coyote, Elliot . . .'

While Curly cursed and screamed, Darrow and Hugh had been taking aim. They fired almost together, both men knowing there was no use in making further demands for surrender. Curly jerked twice, dropping one gun as he staggered, then sank to the ground. He sprawled face down, one outflung hand almost touching his dead horse.

Darrow glanced across at Hugh, who kept his rifle aimed at the still body.

'Check him, then catch me up,' the sheriff ordered. He didn't bother to add a warning that Curly might be playing dead. Hugh's fine instinct for self-preservation made it unnecessary.

Black Elliot had chosen to put distance between himself and the lawmen by continuing on through the prairie-dog town, instead of trying to cut left or right. He had slowed to a steady jog and was watching the ground intently as he wove his horse between the burrow entrances. These were circled by a low mound of earth, which the prairie dogs used for their look-outs, but they still weren't easy to see among the clumps of sage and short grasses. Darrow took up his reins and went after the outlaw, cradling his rifle across his lap. The black trotted out evenly, its head lowered as both horse and rider strove to pick their way between the treacherous holes burrowed in the ground. All the prairie dogs within a hundred yards had vanished safely underground. A couple of the plump, brown rodents stood sentry duty at a distance. Darrow knew that there would be others, further away still. The holes of this town stretched for three or four miles over this piece of prairie.

They rode on, under the bright, hot sun. Every step that the horses took had to be judged; every patch of ground was examined. The horses' hoofs thudded steadily on the short buffalo grass; leather saddles creaked as the riders shifted their weight to help the horses avoid a hole seen almost underfoot. Sheriff Darrow glanced ahead now and again, his dark eyes assessing the ground further ahead and checking on the man he was chasing. On they went, neither man willing to give in; each waiting for the other to make a mistake.

The ground began to slope downwards, encouraging the horses to gain speed. Darrow let his black stride out faster, putting his trust in the horse. Gabriel trotted on willingly beneath him, his black mane blowing in the breeze and his ears pricked. Darrow shut his mind to thoughts of Curly's dead horse and concentrated on closing the distance between himself and Black Elliot.

Up ahead, Elliot didn't dare to look round and find how close the sheriff was. He was fully occupied in keeping his horse balanced as it trotted faster down the burrow-riddled slope. Darrow could see that Elliot's horse was close to getting away from his control as it jogged faster down the slope. He reined in his own at once and lifted his rifle. Elliot was already at long range for the Winchester, but Darrow took the time to adjust the sights and aim carefully. His first shot grazed the rump of Elliot's horse. It squealed and jumped out of its fast, unbalanced trot. The horse landed half on its knees, almost throwing Elliot over its head. Falling downhill, with its rider's weight over its neck, the horse had no chance of making its feet again. It staggered, caught one foot in a prairie-dog burrow, and rolled sideways. Elliot kicked his feet clear of the stirrups as it fell, and landed beside the horse. It was a soft landing, and he was on his knees almost immediately, reaching for the butt of his rifle. He grabbed it as the horse rolled away from him, getting its legs under itself to stand up.

Darrow had started riding forward again as soon as he saw Elliot's horse shy. He kept moving as Elliot's horse struggled to get up, inadvertently placing itself between Elliot and the sheriff. Elliot snatched at the reins, but his horse was clearly lame on its near-hind leg.

Darrow halted his own horse and shouted. 'Throw down your gun and surrender!'

'Go to Hell, white-trash lawman!' Black Elliot answered. He let his horse's reins hang loose to ground-hitch it, and took shelter behind the animal to aim his rifle over its back.

The insult stung Darrow's aristocratic pride but he buried his feelings. He swung his black horse so it was facing directly towards Elliot. The angle would make it a narrow target, and the horse's head and neck would give him some cover. Darrow was gambling that Elliot wouldn't risk shooting Gabriel except as a last resort; with his own horse lame, he needed one of the lawmen's horses to escape and survive on the prairie. He heard the crack of Elliot's rifle and saw a sagebrush torn up just two yards away, almost at the same time. Darrow spoke quietly to his horse, calming it, as he adjusted the sights on the rifle and carefully took aim.

Elliot's next shot passed close enough to make Gabriel snort and toss his head.

'Steady, boy,' Darrow said calmly, steadying the Winchester again. He couldn't see much more than Elliot's head, arms and shoulders.

Another bullet zipped past, so close he heard the crack as it passed his head. The sheriff ignored Elliot's fire, forcing himself to remain calm when every nerve was warning him of danger. Darrow's breathing and heartbeat slowed as he concentrated, aligning the sights and allowing for the ever-present wind that ruffled the prairie. Another bullet cracked past, but Darrow didn't even notice. He steadily applied pressure to the trigger of his rifle, bracing himself for the recoil.

The small puff of smoke from his rifle obscured his narrowed vision for a moment, then Darrow saw Elliot's horse swinging away from the body that slumped against it. Elliot hit the ground face down, his rifle falling from his hand. His horse limped a couple of steps away and halted. Darrow lowered his

Winchester and took a deep, shaky breath. A shout from behind told him that Hugh had reached the top of the slope. Darrow glanced back and signalled for him to come down, then rode slowly to where Black Elliot lay dead.

People in Govan stopped on the sidewalks, and crowded to doors and windows to watch as Sheriff Darrow and Deputy Hugh Keating rode slowly by. Black Elliot's horse limped behind Hugh's, with two bodies tied across its saddle. The lawmen didn't stop to speak, but the bodies were recognized, and word spread fast around town. Hugh had suggested covering the bodies with a blanket, but Darrow had disagreed; the sheriff wanted to impress his authority on Govan, and knew how to achieve it.

By the time they turned into Main Street the news had already reached the sheriff's office. Richard, Louisa and Josh Turnage all came out on to the sidewalk to greet them. Richard approached his brother, looking up at him anxiously.

'Are you all right?' he asked, offering a tin mug of water.

'That poor horse is lame!' Louisa jumped off the sidewalk and bent to examine Elliot's horse. She took no notice of the corpses roped to its saddle.

'We got the other two penned up inside,' Josh told Darrow, indicating the office. 'Richard bowled one of them clean out, the way Louisa puts it. Tomcat got broke a bit, but we called in the doc and he'll mend.' The undertaker studied the two bodies draped over the lame horse. 'I might as well take those two back

154

to the store as they are. There's room in my stables for the horse.'

'Thank you.' Darrow dismounted, and patted his black horse on its hard neck. He unfastened the saddlebags, which contained all the jewellery found with Curly Joe and Black Elliot, and slung it over his shoulder. Darrow passed his reins to Edison, who was leaning on the hitching rail, and told him to take his horse, and Hugh's to the livery stable.

The office seemed refreshingly cool and dim after the glare of the sun outside. Deputy Pacey was at the desk, writing up the arrest of Tomcat Billy and Irish in the logbook.

'Is someone watching them?' Darrow asked abruptly, dropping a pair of saddlebags beside the desk. 'Or am I going to find empty cells again?'

Pacey smiled widely. 'When Doc Travis was tending to Tomcat, he found these rolled up in Tomcat's neckerchief.' He indicated a small cigar-box on the corner of the desk.

Hugh peered into it, and gave an exclamation of delight 'These are beautiful. I wonder where he got them?' He picked out two pieces of metal and studied them for a moment, before assembling them into one lockpick. 'I'll have to find some time to practise with these.' He put the lockpick back in the box, and picked up the box.

'Those are the property of a prisoner,' Pacey objected.

Hugh looked scandalized. 'You can't let a thief keep a set of lockpicks! That's aiding and abetting a crime, surely.' He slipped the box into his jacket pocket before Pacey could think of an answer. Darrow forestalled any further argument by telling Pacey to put the jewellery from the saddlebags in the safe, with the rest that had been recovered from Tomcat and Irish. Then he went to talk to the prisoners.

Hugh followed him to the back of the jail, where the two big cells were. Tomcat and Irish had been put in the same one, leaving the other free for the usual minor arrests that were common in Govan. Irish was sitting on the edge of a bunk, looking more massive than ever in the confined space. He was anxiously watching Tomcat, who was lying on the other bunk. Tomcat's usual spark had gone; his right ankle was heavily bandaged, there was a nasty scrape on his right cheek, and he looked ill.

Irish was the only one of the two to look up as the lawmen stopped outside the cell.

'We caught up with your friends,' Darrow said. 'They're on their way to the undertaker's.'

Irish let out a long breath, and turned his attention back to Tomcat.

'I guess you were after getting the jewellery back, then?' he remarked, still watching his friend.

'I'm sworn to uphold law and order around here,' Darrow drawled. 'You'll both be tried for robbery and attempted murder.'

Tomcat's eyes opened and he half-sat up, his face white.

'Attempted murder?'

'The ambush at the empty shack yesterday,' Hugh said. 'That trap was baited with jewellery stolen at the same time as the items you had.'

Tomcat shook his head. 'No, no. Not a murder sentence an' all.'

'Attempted murder,' Darrow explained, watching Tomcat intently. 'You won't get hanged; you'll get maybe ten years' hard labour; more with the robbery charge.'

'I'd rather be hanged than spend ten years locked up!' The panic in Tomcat's voice was chilling. Irish instinctively stood up and moved towards the lawmen, concern at his friend's fear prompting him to some kind of protective move.

'For sure, you haven't got proof who done that ambush,' he rumbled.

Hugh was watching Tomcat, his soft heart touched by Tomcat's distress.

'I know!' Hugh exclaimed suddenly. 'There's something you could help us with.' He turned to the sheriff, who looked unhappy about hearing one of Hugh's ideas. 'If they help us out, we could drop the charge of attempted murder. No charges have been formally made yet, have they?'

'True,' Darrow agreed warily. 'How do you reckon they can help us?'

Hugh turned back to the cell. Tomcat was staring at him, his green eyes unblinking.

'There's some jewellery that hasn't shown up yet,' Hugh said. 'Where are the tiaras? None of you were carrying them, and we searched this entire bloody town without finding a thing. Where the hell have you hidden them?'

The anxiety left Tomcat's eyes, and his face slowly relaxed into a smile.

'I done buried them one night,' he said, and pointed into the next cell. 'I snuck under the floorboards and buried them right about there.' The smile changed into a broad grin.

It took a few moments for the truth to dawn on Hugh, that part of the jewellery had been almost under his feet all along.

'How did we miss this one?' Hugh gasped. 'I'm sure we checked every damn building in town. I know I didn't do this one, but I thought . . .'

His exclamations died away as he looked at the sheriff beside him. Darrow was laughing for the first time in days. Hugh looked puzzled for a moment, then began to smile as the irony struck him.

'I think that as Deputy Pacey spent his time sitting here, while we were chasing ruffians across the prairie, it's our turn to rest while he does a little job of digging,' Hugh suggested.

Darrow clapped him on the shoulder. 'Well now, I reckon that's a fine idea. And you can tell him yourself.'

Hugh's smile got even wider as he pictured the handsome, young deputy wriggling his way underneath the building, down in the accumulated dirt and debris.

'You know, sometimes you're a real friend,' he said warmly, before adding. 'But don't worry; I won't tell anyone.'

Hugh and Darrow were standing together again the following morning, this time in Govan's church. For once, the sheriff wasn't wearing his badge, but had a buttonhole on the lapel of his frock coat. The church organ was playing quietly, the music mingling with the hushed voices of the waiting guests, and the footsteps of late arrivals. Hugh fiddled with his gold cufflinks and shot an imploring look at Darrow, his best man.

'It is traditional for the bride to be late,' Darrow said quietly. He seemed by far the calmest person in the church. 'And Minnie isn't quite late, yet.'

Hugh nodded, and glanced at Richard and Louisa, who were sitting in the nearest pew. Richard grinned, enjoying his younger brother's discomfiture. He put his arm around Louisa's shoulder, in a possessive gesture. His wife jabbed him sharply in the ribs with her elbow, somehow still maintaining her ladylike poise. The distraction kept Hugh from immediately noticing movement at the other end of the church. The organ music changed and got louder; the voices stilled. Hugh turned the other way and looked along the flower-decked aisle between the pews, to see Minnie and her father, beginning their walk to the altar.

Hugh unconsciously drew himself up, standing as tall as Darrow for once. He wasn't thinking of himself; his attention was entirely on Minnie. The short train of her white silk dress rustled softly as she walked, her arm through her father's and a simple posy of pale pink roses in her free hand. Minnie's face was blurred behind the soft, embroidered veil but it was easy to tell that she was looking at Hugh as she walked. On her head, worn as proudly as a crown, was a pearl tiara that had been stolen six days ago. Minnie spared one grateful glance for Sheriff Darrow, ready to perform a rare duty not demanded by his badge, then she was standing beside Hugh at the altar.

The music faded away, and the marriage service began.